MIKE WATT

PARASOMNIA

DREAMS OF THE SLEEPWALKER

BASED ON THE SCREENPLAY BY WILLIAM MALONE

Encyclopocalypse Publications
www.encyclopocalypse.com

An Encyclopocalypse Book

Copyright © 2026 by Mark Alan Miller.

Based on the motion picture *Parasomnia*, written by William Malone © 2008 by Luminous Processes Ltd. All rights reserved.

Cover design by Amanda Dempsey.

Interior layout and design by Mark Alan Miller.

Printed in the United States of America.

ISBN: 978-1-966037-67-5

Printed in the United States.

PARASOMNIA
DREAMS OF THE SLEEPWALKER

PREFACE

In life there are some things you just have to do. Not because they make financial or logical sense but because you just want to see those dreams come to alive. Parasomnia is one of those dreams.

It really all began because I was up late one night watching the 1920 film *The Cabinet of Dr. Caligari*. As those beautiful images washed over me, I realized there were more untold stories in there. After I turned the film off, new images flooded my head. Images of a sleeping beauty who couldn't wake-up, and a boy who had always loved her. A story of two people who didn't belong in this world and a villainous corrupter that was dead-set on having the girl for himself. These apparitions created a swoon that I couldn't shake.

The full title of the film and story is *Parasomnia: Dreams of the Sleepwalker*, because the film (and now this beautiful novel by Mike Watt) is a dream and a fairytale set in no particular place or time.

Laura and Danny and even Byron Volpe simply are, and have always been.

Making the film was challenging. Finding the right actress to play Laura, our sleeping beauty, was crucial. We auditioned dozens of actresses. When a found Cherilyn Rae Wilson, we all knew she was right.

She's a terrific actress, smart and has a fresh innocence, which was imperative for the part. Our villain, Byron Volpe was played by Patrick Kilpatrick. A great actor I had worked with in a show called *Sleepwalkers* for NBC. That episode was deemed too creepy by the network, which was largely due to Patrick's terrific performance. Danny the other half or our star-crossed lovers was played wonderfully by then newcomer Dylan Purcell. Another great find.

Filming took about six weeks (long for a little indie film) and post-production took nearly two years. This was because the film has over one hundred and fifty visual effects shots. While most films have over a hundred people working on effects... ours had four.

As for this book, I really want to thank Mark Miller of Ecyclopocalypse for his great help and generosity in putting this wonderful edition out. And I also want to thank Mike Watt for his awesome artistry in writing this novelization. I can't thank you both enough.

One last thing. If you haven't seen the film, please check it out. I would ask that you track down the 2025 Director's Cut (which is the one currently streaming) and not the 2008 version. The 2025 version is the way the film was always meant to be seen. I truly hope you like it and this book.

I invite you to find me online, and share your thoughts.

As I mentioned before, *Parasomnia* is a deeply personal film. They say the first rule of filmmaking is never spend your own money.

When it came to *Parasomnia,* I ignored that rule completely.

William Malone
Writer - Director

PROLOGUE

"Do you ever dream that you are dreaming?"

The question echoed in her mind as she woke. Her ex-husband asked her that in her dream.

It had been years since she'd willingly thought of him. Her legally betrothed horror. Her walking nightmare. She'd been unable to escape him even in sleep. Echoes remained of what he did to her. What he made her do to herself. And others.

How long had it been since she'd escaped him? Not by her own efforts, but by way of the State removing him from society? She'd intentionally stopped keeping track. Once he was gone from her life, she'd banished him from her mind. Every now and then, he'd return in a dream.

When he did return, she woke drenched in sweat, gasping for air, clawing at her head to get him out. But this morning's dream was different. She expected his touch to be icy and hard, burning through her flesh and into her skull. Instead, the touch was warm. Almost loving. Almost the way he'd touched her when they first met. Lifetimes ago. Wakefulness chased away the dream, and what was left behind was almost wistful, almost nostalgic, for a time in her life that she knew had never happened.

Their happiness hadn't been real. The spell of dark dreams had been broken the minute the jury declared him "Guilty." Guilty of crimes they could hardly identify beyond their own horror. They believed, in their hearts, they had set her free. The poor wife. That poor woman.

The dream should have left her unsettled, unable to continue with her day. *"Do you ever dream that you're dreaming?"* It had taken a long time, but she finally knew the difference between dreaming and waking. Long ago he had made that difference as tangible as steam, but the State said she was safe from him, the doctors said she was free of him. Put him from your mind. (*Easy for them to say. They didn't have his fingerprints smeared all over their minds.*)

Instead, she felt fine. She was in her own room. In her own apartment. Free. The Monster was far away, he could never hurt her again. She recognized it. She knew it. And she was proud of herself as she slid out of bed.

She showered. Primped. She even pampered herself a little, rewarding herself with a quiet moment of tea on her balcony. Beneath her, before her, the city was waking up to a brilliant orange sunrise, buildings glittering like industrial stars. She was part of it, but still removed, and safe, on her terrace, in tiny part of the world she owned.

Were there anyone to see her, they would think that she seemed happy. Whatever "happy" meant. *Content* at the very least.

As an indulgence, she gave herself an extra half-teaspoon of sugar, and she sipped her tea and watched the city bloom.

On the table beside her hand, her phone began

to buzz and bounce. For a moment, she considered not answering it. She wanted her quiet morning to last. She didn't want to deal with clients, or their problems, or their traumas. She wanted to stay in the gold of the morning.

Her hand moved by its own accord, automata programmed by society to always answer a ringing phone. It was an older phone, it suited her needs, and she flipped it open and held it to her ear without saying a word.

Alone on her terrace, high above the city, there were no witnesses to her breakfast's end. Her expression never even changed. No one overheard the one-sided conversation. No one heard the horrible whispering that seemed to sing to her over the phone. That voice she thought she'd escaped. Her mind churned in tidal waves dread as his words and desires flooded her thoughts. Suddenly a terrifying calm came over her.

She closed the phone, set it down carefully on the table. Taking the napkin from her lap, she dabbed her lips, needlessly perhaps, but it was proper etiquette. The voice told her a secret and then gave her a way out. She *wanted* to do this.

The iron legs of the chair squealed against the terrace's hard wood, but the noise didn't register. Three short steps brought her to the terrace's railing. Another two brought her up to the ledge. She took one more and the city rushed up to meet her.

Time stood still. Madeline's mind raced as the pavement came up to embrace her. A million memories flood her head as the floors of the buildings flew past. It seemed she had forever to think about what was happening. Would this be it? The end of all her pain? Certainly it must be she thought.

Amidst the cries of surprise and shock, pedestrians leaping back to avoid the spreading blood, one passerby couldn't help but take a closer look. He grimaced, slightly ashamed by his morbid curiosity, though he couldn't help but notice how peaceful she seemed. Even as she coughed blood with her last breath, she looked content.

Her name was Madeline Volpe. And now she was free.

ACROSS TOWN AND YEARS LATER: "That's how it ended for Volpe," said Dr. Corso, stubbing out his cigarette and lighting another. He only smoked when he told that story, and then for a few days after. He looked at the squirrelly young man sitting across from him, the desk between them. "So you want to know about our sleepers?" He offered the pack. The young man declined. "Phil." Dr. Corso suddenly remembered the man's name.

Phil reached into his backpack and pulled out an old tape recorder. Something from the '80s with the big push buttons. He attached a little microphone to it by a wire. Dr. Corso felt like he was being interviewed by a time traveller.

"Do you mind if I record this?" Phil asked.

Dr. Corso shook his head. "No, I don't mind."

He started from the beginning…

CHAPTER 1

"Mom, is this where we're gonna live?"

Still groggy from his nap in the car, eight-year-old Danny looked up at the towering house, dirty, ancient, like a witch's tower. He knew why they were there. He hadn't meant to say his question out loud. It was his dream talking.

"No, silly," said mom, turning off the engine. "I've just got talk to the lady who lives here about some make-up."

Danny hated sleeping in the car. He didn't like waking up in a brand new place. But that was what weekends with mom were like. She was The Avon Lady. She drove a pink car and on the weekends, she worked to convince sad old women that they could be pretty again if they bought enough paint.

The closer they came to the house, the bigger it got. ("*Perspective*," his teacher would say, "it changes with distance." He forgot the rest.) There was a small wasp's nest in a corner of the bowing porch roof, the hateful insects just getting started. He squeezed his mother's hand. Only a witch would live in this kind of house. "Is she gonna be a monster?"

His mother's name was Anne, and she answered him with a hand-squeeze back. "Well, I hope not. She just wants to look pretty."

Even though he didn't know yet what the lady looked like, Danny still muttered, "Good luck," and *hmphed* a bit.

It was *Saturday*. He didn't want to spend all day Saturday driving around with mom from one creepy old lady's house to the next. Always dark, always dusty, always always *always* smelling funny. Like the funeral home he'd gone to once. The last time he saw his dad. So dusty you can never get it clean.

Mom never seemed to mind these houses. She dressed up neat and clean—"professional," was her word—and she plastered on her fake Avon-lady smile. It hid the sad one she usually wore. With a final glance down at her son—Danny tried to give her a look of encouragement—Anne knocked on the door with the peeling paint and cracked glass window.

After a few seconds—both Anne and Danny listening for sounds of movement within the dark house—the door swung open and there was an old woman inside. Not as old as Danny had imagined her. Just... he searched for the word... *frumpy*. Like she wore clothes beneath her clothes, topped with a yellowish white sweater wrapped around her shoulders. Maybe mom *could* make her look pretty, but it would take a long time.

Avon Anne snapped into her routine. Danny had helped her practice. "Hi. Mrs. Mulliner? I'm Mrs. Sloan. I'm your Avon representative."

Mrs. Mulliner didn't answer, but she gave Danny a disapproving little stare. Mom Anne picked up on it, and fought her maternal instincts to focus on the sale. She needed another sale. Even Danny knew that. "Oh I hope you don't mind I brought my son along. This is Danny. Say hello to Mrs. Mulliner."

"Hi, Mrs. Mullminer," Danny said, and his mother smiled in approval.

"Be polite, but be charming," She'd coached him.

"What's charming?"

"Just being the best kid you can be."

After a while, he realized that he was another tool to use to win over clients. Some of the old ladies just loved Danny. Those kinds of visits were great, and there were sometimes glass bowls of wrapped candies lying about.

Mrs. Mulliner just grunted and moved slightly to her left. "Come in," she said, and from her tone, Danny knew there would be no candy to be had in this house.

It was dark, as expected. And it had that musty smell he'd expected. The kind of smell a house gets when not enough air gets in. Like that funeral home. That dead person place. Filled with dead people's furniture, looking like something out of those black and white movies that run on TV during the day in the summer. (Even one of those would be preferable to what Danny knew was coming next.)

"Thank you for letting me come over. I have some really great things to show you." Mom was fully in business mode now. She only had one other thing to take care of before she could give the old lady her entire attention. "Would it be OK if Danny waits here?" She indicated a simple chair in the hallway, beside a simple table that one would use to keep a telephone off the floor, before everybody had cell phones.

Mrs. Mulliner didn't smile. Didn't offer him juice or any kind of treat. She barely looked at him as she began shuffling deeper into the house. "Sure. Just tell him not to touch anything."

He sat down unprompted, took his mother's coat as he was accustomed to.

"Sweetheart. I won't be long," Anne said.

I know, he didn't say.

"Just sit down over there and wait for me."

I know.

"And like the nice lady says, don't touch anything."

I KNOW. He gave her a smile.

The Hallway was shaped like a T. Where Danny sat, he could kinda see mom and Mrs. Whatever in the living room. He'd heard her routine—*schpiel*, Mom sometimes called it—so many times, he could repeat it with her. But sitting in the dark hallway, he sat and watched dust motes dance around in a sickly sunbeam.

Mom's voice was both inside and outside his head. *"Here are the moisturizers, and here are the astringents..."*

Booorrrring. He stared at the floor, past his dangling kicking feet. He needed new shoes. Cooler ones.

"And you can see here that it matches just about any flesh tone..."

Danny stared at the ceiling. There were cobwebs in every corner. (*Damned near*, he thought, proud of his internal rebellion.) *This is gonna take forever...*

Something in the corner of his eye moved.

Danny's head snapped to his left, towards a staircase he'd barely noticed, the house being so dim. Something on the landing, up those old steep stairs, was trying to hide between the carved slats of the railing. Craning his neck, straining his eyes to see through the gloom, Danny was only half sure what he'd seen was real. Sometimes he imagined things. Especially on days when he didn't get enough sleep. Danny hated to sleep. The world changes while you sleep.

No, something was definitely moving up there.

Quick, he looked back at his mom and Mrs. Hassenfeffer or whatever, but they were involved with some gross concoction his mother had "specially chosen." He got up—*he wouldn't touch anything!*—and moved closer to a better look.

Tentative steps—like he was approaching a squirrel or a stray cat—Danny mounted the first step, running his hand along the old wooden bannister, worn smooth over the years. (*Epochs*, he remembered from his vocab test.)

This was dangerous. Wandering around some stranger's house. He'd for sure be accused of *snooping*. Climbing one step at a time, heart pounding, keeping his eyes ahead on whatever was moving. *Don't look back, Danny, or the witch will come after you!*

At the top of the stairs, there was a slight bend, just enough to block his view of the mover. He caught a glimpse: bare white feet, some kind of white nightgown... maybe... golden hair? Peering around the bend, Danny was just in time to see a door at the end of the hall quickly close.

There must have been a million doors in that hallway, or at least five. The others were open, leading to bedrooms, a bathroom, all dark, darker even than the hallway. Danny moved towards the closed door.

The carpet was red, but so worn in some places that it had no color at all. There were spare pieces of old wooden furniture sitting beneath old portraits of soldiers. Life was all around him, and still, he thought of the funeral home.

Why are you doing this? His Jiminy Cricket voice demanded. ("Conscience," was the right word.) But Danny was gripped in the thrill of the forbidden. Even this little bit of rebellion was adventure. He needed to meet this stranger. Were they playing with him? Were they scared of him? They were probably told not to talk to strangers either. And he was a stranger, no doubt.

He stared at that closed door for what was probably forever, before he finally gathered the nerve to reach for the knob. He was gonna twist the knob and find the hider and tell them they shouldn't be afraid of him. He was just a kid. Beneath his fingers, the metal knob was so cool, so smooth...

The knob turned in his hand!

Danny stepped back just as the door eased open. Maybe *they* wanted to hurt *him?*

In the doorway was the most beautiful girl Danny had ever seen. Her hair was gold and her nightgown was white and so was her skin and her eyes were big and blue. She looked like she wanted to smile at him, but wasn't sure how.

"Hi," Danny said.

The little girl didn't answer him. She stared at him like he was something she'd never seen before. Not just him, *Danny*, but like she'd never seen another kid before. Without speaking, she reached out and touched his face. He didn't jump back, even though it was a *girl* touching him. He was just as mystified by her behavior. Somehow satisfied, she drew her hand back.

"Hi," he said again. "My name is Danny. What's yours?"

Again, she didn't answer him. Instead, her lovely little face grew the widest smile and her eyes flashed with something Danny couldn't define. Later, he would realize it was called "recognition." But they'd never met before…

She blinked her eyes at him, as if he still wasn't quite in focus, or if he was somehow too bright to look at.

It should have made him uncomfortable. "Can't you talk?"

No answer. Maybe… she wanted him to touch her the same way. To communicate?

Swallowing hard, Danny pursed his lips and reached out to touch the little girl's face. Her cheek was so soft and so much cooler than he'd expected—

The girl's big blue eyes rolled up into her head and she dropped to the floor, like some evil puppeteer had cut her strings. She crumpled into a heap of hair and limbs and Danny's entire body froze in terror.

He couldn't breathe. He didn't dare look behind him. Panicked, he fell to his knees and shook the girl's shoulder. "Wake up… please wake up."

The girl didn't move. "Oh, no…" Danny said, his breath back but only now in gasps. "Oh No, I killed you!"

The girl refused to move. Danny heard his own voice screaming for his mother. He ran so fast down the stairs he nearly tumbled down the last few. His mother appeared at the base and caught him. "I didn't do anything mom! I swear! I just said *hello!*"

Mrs. Mulliner pushed past them and headed up the stairs. She didn't seem angry or even that concerned. She didn't even say anything when she picked the girl up, threw her over her shoulder, and carried her back into that room.

"It's okay," he heard his mom say. "She's okay."

"I killed her!" he wailed.

"No, honey, no," she said, watching the sale fade away.

"YO, DANNY? WAKE UP, MAN."

The world snapped back into focus, the little girl and the old house an almost-forgotten memory, dredged up from who knows where for who knew what reason.

Twenty-three-year-old Danny blinked at reality: He was behind the counter, where he should be, at Andre's Record Collectibles, listening to another of Phil's lengthy lectures on pop culture and history. He was safe, surrounded by acres of vinyl and fellow collectors, historians, and freaks.

Floating above their heads, wafting from speakers too expensive for the store: "My Loving Days Are Through." The Sheffields. Destination Records. November, 1965. B-Side to "Please Come Back to Me."

Danny shook his head to clear the trivia. "Yeah, sorry, what?"

"You need to get more sleep, man," Phil said with his normal hostility. "I asked you if you've heard of Dick Wagner?"

Dick Wagner... Dick Wagner... Danny's brain found the place where that name was stored. "Sure...'70s band called Frost." The world made sense again.

"OK, but did you know that he was in a group from Michigan before that called The Bossmen?"

C'mon, Phil, who do you think you're talking to?

"Yeah, I love them... sort of pseudo-Beatles. I've got original 45s of 'Take a Look' and 'Here's Congratulations'." Immediately, Danny hated himself. He'd yet again taken the bait.

"Yeah, well I bet you don't have the single that's got 'You're the Girl' and 'Wait and See' on it?"

There it was. That smug expression on Phil's face. That *Phil-face*. Phil had a lazy eye that made him seem like he was looking smug in two directions at once.

Still: "Nobody's got that. That's the only record I'm missing from my '60s garage bands. I've tried all over the country... I've got The Plagues, The Five Emprees, The Rationals from Detroit," He could have named ten more.

Phil waved his hand dismissively. "Yeah, well last week I was *in* Detroit to do a piece for the paper, and guess who I bumped into at a record shop? Pete Woodman—the Bossmen's drummer. He's got *extra* copies of all that stuff."

Goddamn you, Phil. "No shit? I've got to have one."

Before Phil could lay out his terms and conditions for acquisition, old Andre knocked on the counter. (*Tweedy*, that was the word for Andre.) "Danny, it's past lunch time... take your break."

Danny nodded, half listening, still thinking about Phil's 45 like it was a Faustian bargain. "Yeah, ok..." More out of habit than anything, Danny glanced at the clock on the register, and an icicle of alarm shot through his chest. "Oh shit!"

"What?" Phil asked, carefully inspecting the edge of a 45. (The Five Emprees, "Little Miss Sad," Freeport Records, 1961).

"Denise!" Danny said, grabbing his coat and bag. "I was supposed to meet her at home for lunch."

"Late again? You're gonna hear about it."

"All I wanna hear is 'You're the Girl'!" he shouted to Phil. "You've got to get me that record." That was his way of saving face as he raced out the door, announcing to the other vinyl-heads that he was still a man of refined taste and culture, and whether or not he still had a girlfriend should be beside the point.

TRAFFIC DIDN'T MAKE things any better. The bus seemed to make extra stops in brand new neighborhoods. And, as usual, the elevator was "Out of Order," as it had been since probably the late '80s. Sweat dripped from his chin as Danny reached the last of the staircases to his floor. Denise and the apartment were just ten yards away. *Just lemme reach them...* He'd promised he'd never let this happen again. It was his fault. It was his sword to fall on. He did *not* want another fight. *Please, God, let her be stoned and chill...*

"Hey, Danny!"

He didn't stop, but he slowed slightly, greeting his nearest neighbor. *How does she always know when I'm coming? It's like she has me under surveillance.* "Hi, Sara. I'm sorry I'm kinda in a hurry."

Sara was an actress, and gorgeous in a high-maintenance way. Like a Victorian fireplace. Today, her attempt to appear casual in a three-hundred dollar sweat suit and tank top ensemble was almost successful as she blocked his way. "I was just wondering if you were moving?"

Boy, she's weird. "No... why?"

Her face grew a positively evil grin. "I just saw your sofa in the alley when I came up, and I thought..."

Oh... crud.

Her little game over, Sara moved aside and allowed Danny access to his front door. His open front door.

He opened it further. His small flat looked so much bigger than it usually did. He suspected it was because much of the furniture was missing. What wasn't missing wasn't in great shape.

He was in shock. Denise had a temper, yes, true. Everyone who knew her had felt her wrath at one point or another. But that's what made her so exciting. Who needed self-esteem when you dated a woman with a body like that... right?

The wreckage she left behind was too obvious for metaphor. At least she hadn't trashed his albums. Or his amp. Just anything personal for the two of them.

Broken glass crunched beneath his foot. It was from the remnants of the framed picture of the two of them when they'd first moved in together. Happy, smiling. Their future filled with hope and wonder and possibility. Instead of poverty, and reality, and insomnia. He'd missed a dozen dates, blown off discussions of therapy. *Therapy? It wasn't like they were married.* It had been bad for a long time, and he couldn't entirely blame lack of sleep. Maybe, subconsciously, he'd wanted this to happen. But that would mean that she was right: that he *did* consider her an afterthought. He didn't want her to be right.

He sifted the photo out of the wreckage, the smiling faces launching him back in time to that day. That very happy day. When they found an arts' district hovel they could both call home. Now it was a cavern of sadness. With a sigh, Danny flipped the picture over. That's when he noticed the brand new writing on the back.

YOU SUCK... love Denise.

He wanted to cry, but he was too tired to produce tears. When was the last time he'd slept? He didn't notice that Sara was still in the doorway watching his deconstruction. He didn't notice when she finally, mercifully, closed the door and left him to sit in his waking nightmare.

CHAPTER 2

The damage was more psychological than physical. She'd stripped every room down to the light bulbs, leaving behind negative space as a pointed reminder to him of what had been his and what had been hers. Everywhere there were piles of records, stacked high and flat, compressing and devaluing. The shelves had been hers. The 45s stored in the closet had been dumped in the old clawfoot bathtub.

Denise had always been an iPod girl. Vinyl was antiquated. She'd always referred to his collection as "hoarding."

Whatever contempt she'd felt, it hadn't extended to destruction. She could have taken a hammer to every album and half of him would have supported her for it. Or, at least, understood. Maybe it was what he deserved. There, on top of a stack of LPs, a single 45: "I Need You"/"Out In The Streets", Capitol pressing, 1968. Did she remember—that was the first album she'd ever bought him. A result of their flirting at Andre's, eight or so months ago. He'd told her it was a favorite and he was thinking of keeping that particular 45 for himself. He remembered the mischief in her eyes as she demanded its purchase. It was almost cruel, but eyes that beautiful could make you ignore cruelty.

When he closed up that night, she met him at the door, album in hand, a kiss print across the sleeve (completely ruining its value). A prank that started a relationship. Hell, even moving in together had been her idea. Then, he sleepwalked into the life she was planning and failed to live up to her expectations every day, in every way.

After cleaning up the glass and debris, Danny decided to cheer himself up by visiting someone worse off than he was. Billy was always good for reminding him what real misery was. Whether he asked or not.

HE DROVE his old Pacer into one of the more depressing ends of the city. Sometimes he felt like the old AMC, as he too imagined he had different-sized doors. Metaphorically. His train of thought dragged with it a wide yawn. The car bounced as he pulled into the parking lot for the Hamilton-Hart Hospital. The Drug Rehabilitation Unit, specifically. You had to be specific just to get the parking pass.

Danny had been there a half dozen times already, but still he followed the arrows and signs to the Rehab building. He couldn't trust his own sense of direction. He successfully navigated the hallways. At the center of the maze, instead of a minotaur, was Nurse Janine.

Nurse Janine could be just as scary as a minotaur though. No matter how many times they'd done their little "Sign In" ritual, she never seemed to remember him. Danny just had one of those faces, he guessed. A visage worth forgetting.

She looked up at him, vaguely, before returning her attention to the forms before her. Even though she sat nearly two feet below his field of vision, somehow it was Danny who felt small. "Yes?" she asked without meaning it.

"Hi... I'm looking for a... patient. Billy..."

She looked up at him again with razor blade judgment.

Danny forced a smile. "...ah, *William* Dornboss?"

She checked the clipboard.

*I'm here almost every day! Almost at the same time every day! I could draw you from memory and you know who I'm here to see! I'm the **only** one who ever comes to see Billy, you hateful—*

But the ritual had its required dance moves.

Nurse Janine began her chant: "Drug rehab. You're not carrying any contraband of any kind? Drugs or weapons?"

To which Danny gave his equally enthusiastic programmed responses: "No. No. No."

Neither were listening. Call/response. A mundane ritual of Polite Society. She never looked up, as she pointed in the vague direction of his destination. They said, in unison, "Down the hall, turn right..." he was around the corner before she concluded, and he'd ceased to exist as far as she was concerned.

If you were making a movie and simply wrote "Drug Rehab Facility" as a location, the Hamilton-Hart Rehab Wing would be exactly what you'd get: drab, lifeless corridors, painted a gray intended to be more soothing than incarceration-inspired, and failing utterly. Not oppressive so much as joyless.

There were always fewer zombie junkies roaming the halls than Danny expected. It was an expensive facility after all, and the zombie junkies preferred the seclusion of their more or less comfortable rooms. Even if they were dark, single-cot furnished, and windowless, at least they were out of the rain.

Danny came to a fork in the hallway. Left or right—why could he never remember? His body wanted to turn left, but his brain had enough juice to focus his eyes on the sign just above his head.

NEUROPSYCHIATRIC WARD.

That Way, the arrow indicated. *Keep going the other way, schmuck*, it further implied.

There, of course, to the right, was Billy's room. Exactly where he'd left it. And apparently Billy was fine with the location as well. Danny reached for the handle and missed. The entire door knob was gone. Danny toed the door open.

As expected, there was his oldest friend in the world, hyper-intellectual, intimidating IQ-having, heroin-addicted Billy Dornboss. The guy who could be anything and refused the call. The guy who could weld garbage into the most whimsical mechanical colossuses (colossi?), instead sat alone in his room, at his small table, beneath a single light bulb protected from him by a thick cage, was good ol' Billy Dornboss. ("Super genius," said the sign held up by Wile E. Coyote in Danny's head.) Billy reminded Danny of John Lennon, if Lennon had always *just* gotten out of bed. And boasted a thrice-broken nose.

Spread across the table before him were all the wing's doorknobs. Possibly every doorknob in the place, who could tell? Billy had one in hand, vigorously polishing the faux brass with a filthy rag. Judging from the spread, Danny guessed he was about half done.

Billy looked up from his obsessively vital task, acknowledgeding his visitor's presence. "Daniel."

"William."

After that came a long bit of awkward quiet. Billy loved awkward moments. One of the benefits of being an educated junkie is being aware that no one can ever anticipate what you're going to do. Although most times, Billy couldn't either.

Billy broke the silence. "Don't you love secrets?"

The question startled Danny, and it gave Danny a little thrill.

Danny looked around the room for a place to sit. Even the bed was covered with knobs. Wait, no… there were a lot of hinges too.

"I guess… I never thought about it."

That must have been the right answer. Billy beamed and almost put down the over-polished knob, but then kept it for punctuation. "I have a lot of time to think these days. Anyway, I was sitting here thinking about secrets… and how they have a kind of power… Something unseen… unknown… That which is about to happen or has happened, and is a dark spot to everyone but the conspirators. I love that, don't you? The magic goes away when you tell someone. Never tell your secrets."

Danny kept his expression neutral but in truth he loved a good Dornboss rant. While he himself had never partaken of Billy's suicide of choice, in their weed and beer days, a good Dornboss screed could last hours. The only thing that could turn him off was a re-run of *Jeopardy*.

"I don't really have any secrets," Danny said.

Billy looked at him for a long moment. "Aw, that's sad."

Danny ignored the bait. "What are you doing?"

Again, Billy gave him a long stare. He held up a can of Brasso. "Polishing," he said, the "duh" implied. That explained the oily smell cutting through the antiseptic lemon-ish scent of the hallway.

Fully knowing the answer, Danny asked any-way. "Where did you get all this?"

Billy shrugged, appreciating Danny's apprecia-tion of the bit. "All over... the building mostly. This one is from... I don't remember where I got this one."

"I thought you couldn't leave the room?"

With as much nonchalance as he could muster, Billy cast a thumb over his shoulder. On the single shelf, in front of stacks of paperbacks, was Billy's ankle monitor, only partially disassembled, but blinking contentedly as if still doing its job. Billy held a greasy finger to his lips. "Secrets..."

"No one gives you shit for doing this?"

Billy snorted, half amusement and half con-tempt. "It's part of the *process*."

The bait wriggled. Danny just nodded and waited for Billy to continue. He never had to wait long. "So what happened?" Billy said, filling the dreaded silence.

"So what happened to what?"

"You and Denise?"

"What makes you think anything happened?"

Billy's erratic polishing picked up speed, the mechanism rattling in his hands. It sounded to Danny like Billy was field-stripping a rifle. "My friend, it's written all over you," Billy said. "I can smell it all over you, man. I can *taste* it. She dumped you. I've seen that look a hundred times... Hell, I've seen that look in the mirror."

Danny merely sighed. He knew what was com-ing. Billy had hated Denise and Denise had liked Billy only half that much.

"Ah, fuck it, man," Billy said. "She had no taste. She dresses like she gathers up her clothes and throws them on in a rage. Half the time she looks like a Wal-Mart exploded near her."

Denise called it "homeless chic," because Denise's friends enjoyed her sick sense of humor. Danny just shrugged. "I like the way she dresses."

Billy cocked his head for a moment, as if trying to hear something in the distance. "Nah, 'Danny and Denise?' Sounds like a bad sitcom. She did you a favor... and why *did* you like her? She hates everything you love."

Me included, Danny didn't say. Instead, "She's beautiful."

"And?"

"And... she was nice to me... most of the time."

"'Nice,' there's a recommendation. What can you do with 'nice'? And she was pretty, all right. Too pretty."

"What does that even mean?"

Billy dropped the doorknob on the table, noisily, pointedly, and gave Danny his most intense junkie stare. "Pretty things always have a tragic end. It's one of the laws of nature... It only serves to make them more beautiful. It would have ended badly." He picked up the knob and resumed his polishing. *Thus endeth the lecture.*

"Sometimes I find you scary," Danny said.

"The truth is scary." Once he was sure Danny was looking away, Billy glanced up at his friend. Danny's sadness registered, piercing through the mania, the current med imbalance, and that eternal gnawing need. Danny might be the only person in the world—other than Billy Dornboss—who actually existed. Empathy stabbed him, but it was quickly murdered.

"Hey, you're taking this too hard. In no time at all, the things that you found so cute and endearing about her would have faded," Billy said. "One morning you would wake up and wonder why the hell she has to wear exactly that shade of lipstick or talk endlessly about something some other boyfriend did to her six years ago. Right now there is some guy telling Taylor Swift that he's sick of her shit."

Nodding more out of habit than attention—there were few things more depressing than one of Billy's "pep talks"—that last bit Danny actually heard. "Taylor Swift?" He'd always thought of Billy like the devil on his shoulder.

"Fucking… ScarJo. Whoever, we don't have cable in here." In spite of himself, Danny laughed. And hell, that was the whole reason he'd come to visit. As twisted as he was, Billy could always cheer him up in some off-kilter way. Eventually. "You're probably right." Having sort of gotten what he'd needed, Danny looked down at his watch. "I better get going. I'm late."

"You're always late."

Danny ignored that. He'd heard it from every person in his life. "When are you getting out of here?"

Billy's eyes hardened, realizing the brief enough visit was coming to its conclusion. He picked up another knob. "A couple days…" He didn't look up again. "Hey on the way out, you should check out the psycho ward down the hall. Very entertaining. There's this guy down there… He's so fucked up." He looked up at Danny, eyes gleaming. He couldn't help himself. Anarchy needed to rise. "They've got this black hood covering his head, and he's all strapped up. It's really creepy."

Danny punctured the bubble of mischief with a dismissive: "Sure."

"Whatever," Billy said.

"I'll come by and see you—"

"When the screws let me out of here?" Billy returned to the polishing. "Just go check out Boss

Creepy. I want a full report. You know, when you
have less time to talk."

"Take care of yourself."

"Enjoy," Billy called back.

Yes, it was passive aggressive, but it still stung.
Danny forced and smile and left Billy with a half-
hearted wave behind his back. He took a step towards the way he came.

And stopped.

Goddamn it. Billy always did know a good time
when he saw it. Danny turned on his heel and continued past Billy's room, hoping Billy had been re-
absorbed into his task and wouldn't see the shame
walk. He quick-hopped past the open door and
continued on. Past the NEUROPSYCHIATRIC
WARD sign

This was as close to thrill-seeking as Danny ever
got. His steps were soft and deliberate, his body
knowing he was entering a forbidden area. Or at
least an area that was none of his business. In the
back of his memory, an 8-year-old Danny snuck up
the stairs of an old dusty house...

A distant *thumping* noise drew him closer to an
open room. It was rhythmic and quiet, yet managed
to imply some manner of violence. Straining to iso-
late the noise from the constant hum of overhead
fluorescents and the beeping of various monitors
(all very futuristic-looking from a 1970's point of
view), Danny didn't hear the security guard come
up behind him. Danny jumped, in fright but the
guard didn't acknowledge Danny's presence at all.
The guard stopped at a closed door and checked
the lock. Then checked the second lock. Then the
third. Finally, saving the worst for last, he peeked
through the porthole window into the room. And
then his entire body shuddered.

Shrugging off his dread, the guard disappeared

around the corner, without a look in Danny's direction. Clearly the security here was slack. Maybe it was an under-funded county hospital or the staff had been there so long they just became complacent. Either way, Danny was relieved that his snooping had gone unnoticed. Saddened that he had wasted a fairly decent performance of "innocently wandering," Danny stepped to the heavily-secured door. The porthole was huge, set just below eye-level. Steel mesh crisscrossed within the reinforced glass. On the other side of the door, the patient side, it was lined with a half dozen heavy iron bars. And *still*, it was practically begging to be looked through.

It almost felt like a violation, but Danny couldn't help himself. He bent his knees. And saw.

It was like something out of a trashy Inquisition movie, filled with torture devices and heresy.

On the other side of the door was a small cell, its walls padded and stained. One stain in particular was fresh, and dripping, and red. In the center of the cell was the "freak" Billy mentioned. The prisoner—for surely this was no way to treat a patient —was brutishly tall and broad. He stood crucified in the center of the room, his arms outstretched at his sides, secured to the walls with heavy straps that also encased his fingers like gloves. He could not lower his arms and he could not touch a visitor. His legs were similarly held in place, tight together, defying easy balance and forcing him to sway. As he swayed backwards, the heavy metal rings of the straps banged loudly against the far wall. As he swayed forward, he slammed his head into the nearest, leaving behind smear after smear of blood, even through the thick black hood covering his face.

On each backswing, the hood lifted from his

face, just a little, each lift giving Danny a flashing glimpse of the face beneath. Pale, maggot-white flesh, and a medieval gag-contraption shoved into the gaping mouth.

This prisoner, if it was indeed a human being, suffered now under a punishment from the mind of Dante. Danny couldn't fathom how this could possibly be rehabilitation, but the tableau made it clear: the doctors here were afraid of this creature. The didn't want him to move or touch or even talk. How the hell did he eat? Who... attended to his bodily needs? Who would be so fucking unlucky to have to get... that... close...?

An explosion of noise shot Danny two feet in the air, sending him scrambling backwards from the locked door and the horrors it contained. His heart pounding, Danny swiveled his head and saw the nurse gathering up her dropped platter of food, cursing herself for clumsiness. Danny couldn't help but add to her misery with an accusatory glance of his own.

Shaking off his irrational terror, Danny turned back to the big door, intending to close the little one. But he couldn't help getting one last peek.

Through the door, impossibly close, the prisoner had managed to half-rid himself of his hood, and his one empty black eye stared through Danny's soul.

"Disgusted" wasn't the right word. A black shark's eye glared out of a giant head, gleaming maggot-white. The horror sent Danny stumbling backwards. It took some awkward shuffling to keep from falling on his ass. Muttering variations of "fuck" under his breath, Danny managed to regain his balance, clawing clumsily for a handrail that was not there.

He backed down the hall a few feet and stopped

to get his footing. He sensed that he had stopped in front of an open door.

His vision was still a spinning when the sleeping beauty came into focus.

That was the only description that fit. The room was no cheerier than Billy's, and it was filled with the steadily beeping devices out of *Dr. Kildare*, but at the center of this room was a girl of maybe eighteen, so still and white and perfect, eyes closed and breathing deeply. Soundly. Asleep.

His only thought was he had stumbled upon a fairy princess.

She lay in her bed amidst a webbing of tubes and wires, connecting her to the many machines, all humming and beeping peacefully, letting the room know that all was normal. She was only sleeping.

Danny took another tentative step into the room, still a little unsteady on his feet. All about the room were little bits of normalcy that would be found in a little girl's room: stuffed animals, coloring books, on the little stand beside her were a couple of bracelets made of junk jewelry. Remnants of her waking world, clearly from when she was so much younger than now.

Hypnotized by the quiet rise and fall of her chest with each deep breath, Danny felt a tug to draw even closer. Her porcelain face seemed so familiar, like he'd met her a lifetime ago. Or in a dream. All he wanted to do was touch her cheek...

"You really shouldn't be in here."

For the third time, Danny jumped nearly out of his skin. The voice belonged to a tall man with a distinguished beard and crisp white coat. He didn't seem annoyed or concerned. It was a statement of fact. Danny *shouldn't* be in there. Yet there he was.

The little name plate below the lapel identified the man as "Dr. Corso," and he reached past Danny to retrieve the girl's clipboard and chart from the foot of her bed.

"Oh," said Danny. "I'm a… a relative."

Dr. Corso peered over his glasses at Danny and shook his head. "No, you're not. She doesn't have any relatives." He made a notation on the chart. "That's why she's here… You just saw her through the door and came in. Didn't you?"

The jig was up. "I'm sorry. I… I was just curious."

Dr. Corso shrugged and returned the chart to its holder.

"I came to see a friend of mine," Danny said, for no particular reason. It was clear Dr. Corso didn't care anything about him. Nor did the nurse who came in behind the Dr, and started fussing with one of the Princess's IV bags.

"Drug rehab?" asked Dr. Corso.

Danny stared at him, still coming out of his trance. "What? Oh, yeah."

Corso nodded. "Would you ask Mr. Dornboss to return the knobs and locks to the doors. It is something of a nuisance… and in some cases hazardous to the patients…"

Her face… Danny was entranced. *Where had he seen her before?* "Oh, sure. He does thinks like that sometimes"

Dr. Corso stared at him. Hard. He nodded towards the open door. "And now if you'll excuse us…"

Danny smiled. He wasn't stupid. He just didn't want leave. Not yet. "I was just wondering, you know, what's wrong with her? She looks healthy. She doesn't look sick."

Dr. Corso's demeanor changed almost immediately. The Sleeping Beauty was his most fascinating patient, and he'd talk about her to anyone willing to listen. Like that, his intruder became an audience. "Well… there's really nothing wrong with her. Except she's asleep."

"Like a coma?"

Corso shook his head. "Not exactly. She has a condition called Kleine-Levin Syndrome, accompanied by *cataplexy*. Generally called *parasomnia*. Are you a medical student?"

"No," Danny said. "Art."

"Thank God for that. Have you ever heard of narcolepsy?"

"Yeah, that's where you fall asleep all the time."

"Well, in Ms. Baxter's case…" Dr. Corso smiled affectionately, "Laura… she's asleep most of her life. The result of an auto accident before she was born. Killed both her parents and left her like… this."

"And she can't wake up?"

"She does wake up occasionally, for a few minutes at a time. We never know when or for how long. It's an interesting phenomenon… and rare. She's really only lived a small portion of her life."

"I can't imagine what that is like… Living your life in bits and pieces. It must seem like being in a time machine."

Dr. Corso nodded, clearly losing interest. His patience was sure to go next. "I suppose…"

Laura Baxter.

Danny could feel Dr. Corso's eyes burning through the back of his head. It was just so hard to look away from her. Finally, Danny snapped back to reality. Corso was staring at him. So was the nurse. Laura remained asleep.

"Will you excuse us?" The doctor insisted.

"Sure," Danny mumbled, and shuffled out of the room.

On his way out, he had to go past the monster's

room again. The prisoner had resumed his rhythmic ritual of rattling and banging. Danny hurried past the door without risking a second peek.

He didn't see the rivulets of blood running from under the prisoner's hood and down his chalky white neck. Nor did he see the man slam his head into the wall—padded or no-as the prisoner whispered, softly, and laughed.

CHAPTER 3

For her entire life, Laura Baxter lived in two different worlds: Hospital and Lauraland.

Lauraland was bright and sunny and happy all the time. She lived in a big house with a Mom and Dad. There was a great big yard and trees all around, plenty of room for puppies and kittens to play together and never fight. There was always a rainbow in the sky and it didn't hurt to look at the bright, smiley sun. She was happy there. She was safe there.

Hospital was different. There were always people in white, standing over her, poking and adjusting and stabbing and hurting.

You couldn't really *feel* anything in Lauraland. She knew the kittens were soft and the ice cream was cold, but her hands didn't really feel like they held anything. Pain didn't hurt there. And Mom and Dad didn't really have faces. Mom died while Laura was still inside of her. But Laura loved them both and in Lauraland, they were still perfect.

None of the flowers or candy rivers had a smell or a taste. She just imagined they were sweet and happy. Hospital had a pungent, and sometimes that smell drifted into Lauraland. When the smell came to Lauraland, she always found herself in Hospital.

Hospital always changed. That's how she knew she was dreaming. She "woke up" in rooms different from when she went to sleep in Lauraland. Although, she couldn't remember ever falling asleep in Lauraland. She just blinked her eyes and poof! Gone was the grass and rainbows. Replaced by flickering white light and masked people and pain. Scary.

The people in Hospital tried to talk to her, to explain that Lauraland was her dream world, and that Hospital was the Real World. But she had no idea what the Real World was like, except for how it was different from Lauraland. It was just a dream, she told herself. "You *dream* you're in Hospital. It's just a nightmare."

In Hospital, there were needles, but there was no Mom, no Dad. In Hospital, there were strangers with papers covered with words. In Lauraland, she knew her ABCs. The best thing about Hospital was that sometimes *Sesame Street* was on the TV in the corner. But in Lauraland, the letters never stayed still as words. Numbers, too, jittered around like bumblebees and didn't really matter. In Lauraland, she danced and was happy.

Sometimes in the Hospital dream, things were good. There was Shelby. Shelby was another nurse, but she wore a sweater all the time over her blue pajama uniform. She'd bring Laura toys and books, for those moments when she was awake enough in Hospital to understand. Laura liked Shelby's voice, and the funny way she said 's' sounded like 'th'. Shelby would sometimes sing to Laura, and then she'd be back in Lauraland.

In Hospital, it was either too dark or too bright and she could never really move well or else the wires and tape tugged at her skin, and other tubes were put *inside* of her. It was terrible. She preferred Lauraland.

One day—She really didn't know when or what *days* were—she found herself in Hospital and was annoyed. People were coming and going and making noise outside her little room. They were upset about someone. The people in white and the bigger people in blue pajama uniforms were pushing and pulling and fighting against one man, who was bigger than all of them. His head was covered and Laura couldn't see his arms. There was some sort of fabric wrapped all around him, covering his arms and holding them tight against his body. He looked like a giant worm.

Laura knew what worms were but she didn't think she'd ever actually seen one.

The biggest man didn't want to go where the other people wanted him to go. He made a noise like he was screaming, but the hood over his head muffled the sound.

The people in white and blue finally dragged the big man past her open door and they took the noise and shouting with them. Somewhere outside her room, she heard another door close. Since Hospital held no interest for Laura, she went back to Lauraland.

Only this time...

Lauraland was gone.

The sun was gone. There were no rainbows. It was a place of howling wind. *Cold*. How could she feel cold?

She couldn't even tell the sky from the ground. Everything around her was dark. Somehow, she knew the dark was also... *sharp*. Mommy and Daddy were not in the dark. Her big old house, her yard, her trees, everything was gone.

In its place was a vast landscape of ash. Hundreds of polished-metal panels the size of doors hung in the air, rotating rhythmically. They were constantly shifting black mirrors, and they created and recreated an endless maze. The rotating mirrors were silent as they moved, but they reflected the noise from the wind, redirecting the gales with each configuration.

Ahead, she saw there was *one* tree. Far off in the distance: an old towering tree, dead forever. Lightning lashed at it, showing off its twisted shape. Inside the tree, there was a house. And inside the house... Laura didn't want to know. She didn't want to go there. Where was *her* house?

Something behind her skittered in the dark, joining other skittering things. She saw things with teeth but no faces. Like their faces had been peeled right off over their skulls. Everything—*everything*—was wrong. All around her, danger. Everything meant her harm.

Panic rose in Laura's chest. She couldn't breathe—how could this be?

Backing away from the things in the shadows, Laura tried to make her way into the maze of mirrors, desperately avoiding the rotating panels, certain they could cut her or burn her or 'lectrifry her. She was certain, no matter what they did, she would *feel* it.

She ran. The ground was hard and cold against her bare feet. Gone was her beautiful dress. In its place was the gown from Hospital. She didn't want that gown—she *hated* that gown. It left her exposed and vulnerable and—*where were mommy and daddy?*

One of the panels swiveled, revealing her reflection. Laura stopped and saw herself. She was so tall! She was so... grown up. She wanted to reach out and touch the beautiful lady in the mirror.

But the lady in the mirror—who looked like how little Laura had always imagined she'd look when she grew up—had something behind her.

There was a big black worm, writhing and growing taller and taller. It didn't have a face, just a big black cone on top. It swayed and swayed and then it shed its hood.

The big black worm had a face.

The big black worm told her its name.

The big black worm had eaten Lauraland. Now it wanted to eat her too.

Run, it whispered. *Tick…tick…tick…*

She ran. She ran so hard and fast. Her feet were freezing cold and the ground was hard and sharp and *what was this?*

Lightning flashed and somehow, she knew, there was a Thing in the House in the Tree, and it wanted her. It wanted to *do things* to her.

A pair of metal panels parted like swinging doors, revealing a stone column behind them. Something was growing out of the stone, its black flesh and bones had webbed out and wrapped around the stone, like moss, or something seeking comfort. Something bad.

The mass of tissue and bone began to move, and from the mass grew a head, bones cracking, muscles snapping, as the head turned to look at her. It looked at her with the face of The Worm.

Laura screamed, and she found herself back in Hospital, still screaming, but making no noise, just a raspy, gasping breath.

Behind her, something was banging against her wall.

…thump…thump…thump…

CHAPTER 4

Some years ago, Danny traded sleep for obsession. Maybe "trade" wasn't the right word. It just happened. Something in his kidhood made him distrust sleep. And that "something" was his mom. Mrs. Anne Sloan, the Avonlady. Because of the way she liked to work, it wasn't uncommon for Danny to go to sleep in his own bed and wake up in a coat and boots in the back seat of the old car. It felt to his young mind that he was some sort of unwilling time traveler.

He didn't have the words for it then, but he hated that kind of "vulnerability." If he could sleep so deeply his mother could not only transport him somewhere, but shove him into his heavy clothes, someone else could do *anything* to him.

He had watched the shows on HBO. He knew there were awful people in the world. So Danny trained himself to sleep lightly. When High School hit, so did hormones and distractions, insomnia was less of a concern. Now it was just habit. If he was out for three hours in a row, he woke up in a sweaty panic. *Was there someone there? Where was he? What's familiar?*

Sleep came easier when he was in a relationship.

A familiar body next to him was an anchor to reality. He didn't sleep *better*, but at least he avoided a panicky awakening. Maybe that's why he'd stayed with Denise as long as he did, long after they stopped really getting along.

Insomnia was something Billy and Danny had bonded over as wild-eyed youths. For distraction, they'd turned to *Trivia Pursuit* and hundreds of VHS tapes of *Jeopardy* Billy had taped for his grandfather when he'd gotten Alzheimer's. Some nights, when Danny stayed over, they'd have to turn the TV way up to drown out Nanna Dornboss's weeping.

Because of this, Danny's brain was a broken television, constantly skipping between stations, with all the white noise in between. When he read about people who didn't have interior monologues, he couldn't fathom that kind of peace.

Lately, his thoughts had managed to fine tune to a single channel: Laura Baxter.

She was living his nightmare, completely at the mercy of the Waking World. Yet that beautiful slumbering face seemed so content. Trusting. Because what choice did she have?

> *"Parasomnias are a category of sleep disorders that involve abnormal movements, behaviors, emotions, perceptions, and dreams that occur while falling asleep, sleeping, between sleep stages, or during arousal from sleep."*

So said Wikipedia.

> *"Parasomnias are dissociated sleep states which are partial arousals during the transitions between wakefulness, NREM sleep, and REM sleep, and their combinations."*

Furthermore, the 3rd and so far latest edition of the International Classification of Sleep Disorders (ICSD) reported—

"uses State Dissociation as the paradigm for parasomnias. Unlike before, where wakefulness, non-rapid eye movement (NREM) sleep, and rapid eye movement (REM) sleep were considered exclusive states, research has shown that combinations of these states are possible and thus, may result in unusual unstable states that could eventually manifest as parasomnias or as altered levels of awareness."

"Kleine-Levin Syndrome (KLS) is a rare neurological disorder characterized by recurring episodes of excessive sleepiness (hypersomnia), cognitive and behavioral changes, and, in some cases, hypersexuality and increased appetite. These episodes can last for days or even weeks, with periods of normal function in between...

"Cataplexy is a sudden, brief loss of muscle control, often triggered by strong emotions like laughter or surprise. It's a key symptom of narcolepsy, a sleep disorder..."

"For further reading, click the following links. For the film of the same name, please see..."

Danny closed his laptop, got out of bed, intentionally did not look at his clock. He didn't want to know how late it was, or how many hours he had to pretend to sleep before he had to leave for work. Bare feet slapped against bare floors—*my god, her crummy faux Persian carpet had been so warm*—and he went into his bathroom. It took a few minutes of sifting through the 45s in the tub, but he finally found one that suited his mood, or the mood he'd wanted to suit, and maybe this would help.

Denise hadn't damaged his player, left the needle alone. Not every ex would have been so thoughtful.

While The Bossmen sang "Bad Girl," Danny flopped back down on his bed, tried to quiet his mind.

Denise had taken her curtains with her. The streetlight in the park across the road lit up his room and gave him a magic lantern show, tree limb shadow puppets danced across his wall and ceiling. The shadows seemed to merge, granting itself form. The form was… there was no other word for it: *sensual.* The curves and waves were like a young woman dancing. She was not quite in step with The Bossman, nor did she seem particularly bad.

If she had a face, it would be Laura's.

At that, he fell into a dreamless sleep.

AFTER THAT, his waking life felt surreal and dreamlike. Classes were on Fall break, so his routine deconstructed to Work and Home. Get up, go to work, sell people records, come home. Breaking up the monotony was exhausting. Any idle time had his mind wandering back to Laura.

Parasomnias… altered levels of awareness… Springsteen is under "S"… the shadows are dancing… Unlike before, where wakefulness, non-rapid eye movement, and rapid eye movement sleep were considered exclusive states… did I get my grades, Laura Baxter?… research has shown that combinations of these states are possible… I wish I could show you the world… and

Enraged honking snapped Danny out of his trance. The Pacer had stalled while he idled at the light. Angry—at himself, at the assholes behind him—he gave the key a savage twist while frantically waving at them to "go around!"

Once the car coughed back to life, his anger dissolved and his smile returned. Two more blocks, and he turned into the Hamilton-Hart visitor's parking lot and took his ticket.

All the door handles on Laura's wing had been returned. When was Billy getting out? Danny couldn't remember. He wasn't there for Billy anyway.

Fortunately, Billy's door turned out to be closed, so Danny didn't have to worry about it one way or the other.

There was no giant guard around. No Dr. Corso. No one to question his presence in Laura's room.

He slipped quietly inside, and there she was, just as she'd been. Silent, eyes closed and skin glowing beneath the fluorescents, hands at her sides, buried beneath tubes and wires, surrounded by concerned machinery. Her face, even under the ugly feeding tube snaking into her nose, was so beautiful. And yet, something was different. He didn't yet know what.

"Hi, Laura."

Danny didn't know what he expected, but Sleeping Laura remained silent. "I'm Danny... Danny Sloan... I was here before. You... you looked kinda lonely... I thought maybe you might like someone to talk to you."

Still nothing. Of course, still nothing.

"They have you hooked up to a lot of stuff. Do you really need all that? I guess you do."

Something happened then. Laura's body twisted, just a little, maybe a response but probably... not. Still...

There was a chair in the corner of the room, probably for observation. Corso said she never had visitors, had no family... Danny grabbed the chair and swept it over to her side, suddenly very giddy.

"I thought maybe we could talk. You don't have to say anything really... just listen." Danny felt self-conscious and sublimely stupid. He couldn't think of what to say next. *Moron!* "Uh... I'm not sure what to talk to you about. I guess I'll just tell you about the things that you've missed... you being asleep, you've missed a lot of cool things, I bet. Well, like... um... like ice cream."

Laura's hand twitched. Probably involuntarily. Still...

"Oh, uh... Maybe you've *had* ice cream. Or ... oh, going to the beach or a fall day... or The Beatles... you've missed The Beatles... and Nine Inch Nails and Van Gogh... and Beethoven... or maybe you have heard them and you don't know?" A new thought occurred. "Huh, but then again you've probably never heard of Hitler... or atomic bombs... or Teletubbies. I guess there are some good things about being asleep."

He smiled down at her and she slumped-just a little-in response, her head falling off the pillow.

"You don't look comfortable," he said. *Put on a sweater, your mom is cold.* Gently, he lifted her head and adjusted her pillow. Her scalp was so warm against his palm, but her skin was cool. She was as still and beautiful as an Hellenistic statue.

"I wonder what goes on in your head. You must be dreaming... What do you dream about if you don't know a lot of stuff? I'm sorry, I know you're not stupid... they told me you are pretty bright... What happens when you wake up?"

"She's usually disoriented," said a voice behind him. "Does the doctor know you're in here?"

Danny didn't jump. He looked over his shoulder at the nurse he'd seen before with Dr. Corso. "I'm just... talking to her. She looked kinda lonely."

Instead of ejecting him, the nurse seemed to size him up then. Her hard features softened. "Yeah, I guess she is."

Danny watched as the nurse fussed around Laura, checking tubes and numbers, making sure the machines were making the correct beeping noises. Her name plate identified her as Nurse Evans.

"Do you look after her?"

Nurse Evans nodded. "For the last few months. Mrs. Shelby looked after her before that."

"Was she a relative?"

"Just another a nurse here. She was very old. She died. Heart attack. It was kind of sad for Ms. Baxter here."

"Why?"

"Well, because Mrs. Shelby spent a lot of time with her. When she'd wake up, Mrs. Shelby would teach her things." Nurse Evans picked up a stuffed bear from the small pile on the table. "All this stuff, things that she brought in for her. Mrs. Shelby used to say that Ms. Baxter was a quick learner. Well... I don't really have the time..."

That last bit annoyed him. "What does she say when she wakes up?"

Nurse Evans didn't answer right away. She stared down at Laura—Ms. Baxter—with an odd smile. "Just things... She's an innocent. Whatever you say she takes at face value." The smile vanished and the dutiful no-nonsense face returned. Nurse Evans went about tucking and checking and adjusting. "That's why you have to be careful of what you say to her."

Danny understood that was for him.

The Nurse's demeanor changed yet again. She puffed herself up and tapped on the hanging saline IV bag. "There are some research doctors who are very interested in her case. They've been talking about her a lot lately."

And then... Laura moved. Her hand shot out and seized Danny's wrist. Her grip was surprisingly strong, and it told him, "Don't leave."

He swallowed hard. "Um... she's—"

Nurse Evans found no miracle in the motion. "Don't be too concerned. She moves about a lot while she sleeps."

Laura's face was no longer a mask of peace. The expression she wore was almost pleading. Her eyes were squeezed shut. Something was happening with her.

"Is that why she's strapped down?"

Dutiful Nurse Evans shrugged, completely ambivalent. "I guess. You'd have to ask the doctor." She was down to unnecessary movements now. Her job was done. "I think it's probably time for you to leave. I have to give her a bath."

Danny nodded and tried to step away. Laura's grip did not relax.

On a schedule, Nurse Evans pulled them apart and dropped Laura's arm to the bed. "You can come back and talk to her again. Just clear it with Dr. Corso first... OK?"

The "OK?" wasn't a question. Still nodding, Danny backed out of the room, his eyes fixed on Laura's pained expression.

CHAPTER 5

"THEY TRIED TO MAKE ME GO TO REHAB, BUT I SAID no, no, no," Billy sang. Rehab was over. It was his first day of freedom, and he parked his car at a deliberately cock-eyed angle across from Danny's building, traffic flow be damned. Plus, he hated the song he was currently singing and someone needed to be punished for putting it in his head.

He always felt great after a few weeks of sobriety. It meant his backslide would be all the more exciting. Get as close to that original *kick* as you could get. Yeah, drying out always sucks, but a little suffering made one a better man. "I fought the law and the *law won*," he sang, as off-key as Joe Strummer, feeling punk again. He was just swimming in his old leather jacket. Rehab must've cost him ten pounds and it wasn't like he had the mass to spare.

"One of the great side-effects of heroin body," Billy told his last shrink, whose name he'd spitefully never bothered to remember. "Of course, you slam a door too hard, I'm gonna flap around the room."

"Saturday night's all right for fightin'," sang Billy, his brain skipping grooves. Outside the shitty walk-up, Danny's mailbox was the only one over-flowing. "Fucking Sloan, man. Get your shit together."

As usual, the security door was wide open, so Billy bopped right in. Past the usually-broken elevator, past the two little kids on the stairs that nobody knew who they belonged to, past the little old lady of indefinable racial make-up, sweeping her welcome mat while boiling a goat for dinner, if the smell was any indication. Follow along the broken tile, try to ignore the black mold in the corners. The whole world is a death trap and none of us get out of here alive.

"Who wants to live forever, anyway?" he asked no one and got no response.

Reaching the landing, Billy rounded the corner, hoping that Danny's hot neighbor might be exercising in her undies with the door open again. Chick had *zero* shame and Billy liked that in a woman. Nope, closed door. No *chica en casa*. Whatever, getting off heroin made it harder to get hard than when you were on the shit. Or so went his experience.

Billy leaned his whole palm on the buzzer button. With his other hand, he pounded all of Danny's mail against the door. "In, in, let me in!"

There was a series of unlocking sounds, part of the music of city living. Dude had *too many doorknobs*, and that was just a fact of life. The Danny in the doorway was in striped boxers and an old *Siouxsie and the Banshees* t-shirt and didn't even greet him. He just shuffled aside and allowed Billy access to the apartment furnished in late century poverty. No chairs. No tables, except for the entertainment center bearing the turntable and television. Rehab had been fancier.

Billy slapped the fistful of mail against Danny's chest. "Your correspondence."

Further in, Billy surveyed the pathetic scene with better clarity. This wasn't just a case of Denise Withdrawal. He knew Depression when he saw it, and this was giving big-D energy. "Are those records in your fucking bathtub?"

Danny moved past him and closed the privy door.

"Dan, I got sprung and this is how you greet me? See, just thought I'd come by…" Billy's words dried up in his mouth, his brain just noticing what was filling his ears. "What the hell are you listening to?" He didn't actually hate it, but he wasn't about to let Danny know that.

"The Plagues," came the mumbled response to the rhetorical question. "Local band from Michigan. 1965."

He spoke like a sleepwalker. Billy was almost impressed. Who knew Danny had this kind of depth? Respect. He watched as Danny sorted his mail, filing most of it in the circular receptacle. His face changed upon opening the big padded envelope. A gift from Danny to Danny? You always hurt the ones you love, but sometimes you love the one you're with. Or whatever. It was another "new vintage" record and Danny was pleased as a pig in shit.

"Oh, fuck, Denise left a beanbag chair!"

Billy plopped down and the chair *floofed* beneath his skinny ass. Some white ticking farted out with it.

"Love theme from *The Sorrow and the Pity*, 1945, originally recorded by Adolf and the Brownshirts," Billy said. "Sung in the key of M. You're a Crack Ho. What do you have to drink?"

"Maybe some Black Cherry sodas."

It took Billy two tries to free himself of the bean-bag's hearty embrace, and his knees popped as he got to his feet. He decided to take that out on Danny as he went to the fridge. "What happened to all your cool furniture, Tyler Durden? Oh yeah, Denise, right?"

Danny didn't take the bait. He did take a soda from Billy, forcing ol' Dornboss to dive back into the fridge to retrieve one for himself. Danny cracked the can open. "So when did they let you out?"

"What time is it?" Against his better judgment, Billy plopped back down into the beanbag, leaving Danny a milk crate to sit on. No regrets.

"I bet you're glad to be out of there," Danny said.

"I don't know, I was starting to like that place. It suited me. The psycho ward was sweet. There's a lot of really intense character studies in there." Which was true. Nutbags really knew how to bring the chaos. "I'd like to go back and paint some of the really fucked up ones. There was this guy, Shaky Jake... got some kinda weird virus in his head... now his brain is completely hollow. Walks around singing Ricky Martin songs. He starts from album one. You don't dare stop him or he'll start all over again. If I hear 'She Bangs, She Bangs' one more time, I'll slit my throat—Oh, speaking of that. Did you check out their genuine serial killer?"

"The guy in the padded cell."

"No, the janitor who restocks the catheters. Yeah, Big Creepy. Okay, so one of the orderlies told me his story. So get this. The guy used to be a rare book dealer and mesmerist."

(*"Mesmerism, also known as Animal magnetism, is a theory invented by this German doctor in the 18th century."*

"Who was Franz Mesmer?")

"Okay," said Danny.

"He was arrested after hypnotizing his girl-friend and ordered her to jump off a building. At trial, he got the prosecutor to park his car on the Metro-Rail tracks... *Twenty-three* fucking people died. One hundred and three motherfuckers injured."

"That's not true."

"It's *totally* true. Remember about four years ago—the last time you slept for more than ten minutes—Remember the big train derailment?"

Danny shrugged. "Yeah."

"The work of Byron Volpe."

"That can't be a real name."

"Ha. Apparently, he's got these *crazy eyes*." Billy made a face. Danny didn't laugh and that annoyed him. "They have to keep 'em covered up."

Danny just nodded. "I saw 'em."

"You saw the crazy eyes? Fuck you, no you didn't."

"Just for a second."

Billy stared at him, dialing up his Bullshit Meter, but the needle stayed out of the red.

Danny slurped his soda. "If this guy is so dangerous, why isn't he in prison?"

"Some kind of bullshit legal wrangling. He's been there for a long time... Conflicting psych evaluations or something. They say he's some sort of genius."

"He's not much of a genius if he's locked up."

"See *that's* his problem, he's too smart. I've always said it. Stupid people have it made."

"Stupid people?"

"And ugly people. Don't look at me like that. You can't handle the truth. See, if you're too smart or too beautiful, you draw too much attention to yourself, you stand out too much. If you're a little thick or your face was kissed by a semi, you can sit there on your front porch and watch life just go by." He sat back and spread his hands—your honor, the prosecution rests. "Like you're watching a tennis match." Further punctuation, bobbing his head left, right, left, clicking his tongue in rhythm. "It's beautiful."

It was clear to Billy that he'd lost his audience to a beat-up Rubik's Cube. Unsolved after all these years. Another reason for Denise to have dumped Danny's ass. "Which reminds me," Billy said, master of non-sequitur. "Did you see Sleeping Beauty?"

That got Danny's attention. He dropped the Cube and fixed Billy with an odd look. "What do you mean?"

Billy felt a sudden surge of power. He smiled with all his teeth. "The hot little creampuff in the room next to Ted Bundy."

Danny's posture could only be described as "hostile."

"You went in there?"

What, did you have dibs? "Yeah, I went in there. And apparently you did too." Billy studied Danny's face. It was tense, bothered. All the more reason to keep poking the bear. Danny was hilarious when angry. "Good looking babe. Weird about her though, don't you think? Being asleep all the time." There it was. Danny's ears were flushed crimson. "But then again," Billy went on, grin as evil as he could make it, "it makes her kind of the perfect girl. Women are mostly decorative anyway and the one's that aren't are just too much trouble." Danny wasn't even looking at him now. "Still, it would be interesting to see what she'd have to say for herself if she woke up—"

Danny whirled and suddenly there was a finger pointed in Billy's face. "Leave her alone, OK?"

Fuck, this is serious. Billy dropped the evil act. "Hey, Danny. What's going on here? What have you gotten yourself into?"

Danny didn't answer right away. He dropped his arm and his whole body slouched, in a desperate performance of "casual." "Nothing. It's just that they said you have to be careful what you say to her."

Uh huh. "Don't worry... I like them a little more, you know, *lively* myself. She's all yours." Billy couldn't help himself. The evil returned. "At least for another couple days."

"What do you mean?"

"I heard some shrinks talkin'. They're shipping her off to some lab. Gonna make a science experiment out her... like Frankenstein." Billy seized up and did a parody of electroshock. "*Bzzzzz.*" Then, he sang, "'She blinded me with science...'"

That was a deep cut, Billy thought. And Danny really should have appreciated that more. Instead, he just stood with his mouth open like a goddamned empty puppet.

CHAPTER 6

THE ELEVATOR ANNOUNCED ITSELF WITH A LITTLE *ding*. The doors opening to reveal a wide-eyed Danny in the recovery ward made Nurse Evans jump half a foot.

"Excuse me. Hi," Danny said.

Nurse Evans *almost* swore. "You're the one who came to see our sleeping girl."

"That's what I wanted to talk to you about." He lowered his voice, lowered his head, tried to entice her and aid in his noble mission. "Is Laura Baxter going somewhere? I heard that she was getting moved?"

She didn't have time for this. He wasn't a relative, nor was he the first "concerned young man" that turned up at the sleeping girl's room, though it had been a long time since the last. Laura Baxter wasn't the celebrity she'd once been. She opened her mouth to brush him off but then her pager went off. Dr. Corso, again. Likely because that vile Dr. Bhyle was on his way. Speaking of Laura Baxter and her own personal Dr. Frankenstein. Dr. Mengele... *Things she couldn't say out loud...* thought Nurse Evans.

Suddenly, the boy's very existence lost meaning.

"Just wait here a minute. I'm going to talk to the doctor right now."

She heard him call after her: "Can't you just tell me?"

"I said *I'll be right back*." She said to the space behind her. Prince Charming would just have to wait.

STRESS SQUEEZED at Danny's chest. Nurse Evans was gone and no one else coming or going paid him the slightest bit of attention.

Screw it, he would use it to his advantage. That's what *Billy* would do. Or tell him to do. He knew where to go and which color line on the wall went where. Yellow lead to Laura. Maybe for the last time.

Much to his relief, the rehab wing was as quiet as it ever was. Some loiterers in their doorways, one pretending to smoke. No nurses coming or going. No guards. Danny took a deep breath and told his heart to slow down. It didn't listen.

In point of fact, it beat even harder as he approached the closed door with its heavy locks. A punishing cell, not a rehabilitating room. Behind that door was Byron Volpe. Serial killer and hypnotist. (*'He's a hypnotist... a hypnotist of lay-dees,'* sang They Might Be Giants.) Danny felt a long-dormant need to cross himself as he passed the closed door.

For no reason, his feet stopped moving. He froze in mid-stride, then turned back to the closed door again. The locked door. Volpe's door. *Why am I reaching for that window? Why am I opening the window? What is that whispering? What is he saying?*

There was no rational explanation—Danny

watched his hand reach out and slide open the portal, he felt himself look inside.

Still hooded, still akimbo like the thief to Christ's left, Volpe was already looking at Danny. Eyes hidden but still burning through the black cloth, glaring into Danny's brain. Danny could feel something clawing in his skull.

No. Not "clawing." Something was squirming against a scab he'd forgotten about. A wound that had healed over was bleeding again. Like... worms...

Byron Volpe rocked his head back and forth, working his face free of the hood, revealing his nose and gagged mouth. The gag was made of thick leather and metal, set to go into and over his mouth. It was moving. With another crane of his neck, Volpe worked some slack into the gag. The rest, he pushed free of his mouth with a fat gray tongue. The tongue glossed saliva over the thin lips, which then pulled back into a grotesque parody of a smile. Again, the tongue waggled. *Like a big gray worm...*

Danny could feel the hooded eyes, just as clearly as if he could see them.

The voice that came from that cavernous mouth was surprisingly smooth, deep, almost soothing, which was the ultimate cruelty. "A poem by Byron Volpe..." The creature cleared its throat in an almost charming way. "The wanderer stopped... to turn over a rock... the rock gave way... and what was below... ruined his day."

Again, the tongue shot out like a snake's, licking the air. Then Volpe turned away to stare at the browning bloodstain on the padded wall. He'd created his own Rorschach test: *What do you see in my blood?*

"Leave her alone pussycat..." Volpe said. "She's mine in time, in time... she's mine... Tick, tick, tick,

tick, tick, tick, tick." A new rivulet of blood trickled down the side of Volpe's nose and into the corner of his mouth, and that terrible gray tongue lapped at it. "Tick, tick, tick…"

Danny slammed the portal door closed again. He slapped it with his palm to punctuate his resolve. Once the door was closed, he couldn't feel the picking in his brain any longer. That was enough to strengthen his illusion that he'd somehow "won." Moving freely towards Laura's room meant that he'd broken free of Volpe's spell. He needed that to be true.

Laura's door was open. The little light above her bed bathed the sleeping girl with an almost angelic glow. *Jesus, Danny…*

For the second time that day, Danny felt his body move without his participation. Slowly, he went to her side and sat in the chair beside her bed. "Hi, Laura. It's Danny, I've come to see you again. I'm not sure how much time we have. I just wanted to see you."

Maybe it was the light or just wishful thinking, but Danny was sure he saw the corners of her mouth tug just a little. "Are you smiling? I wish I could make you laugh."

Thud. Thud. The wall behind Laura's bed shook just a little. Just enough to be noticed. Volpe banging his head to make his presence known.

Laura's smile vanished, replaced with unease that made Danny's heart hurt. "Just ignore that," he told her. "Here, I brought you something."

Rummaging through his bag, he pulled out his portable CD player and a little pair of speakers. Carefully, he arranged it all on her side tray table. The CD was already loaded, waiting for him to press PLAY. Mussorgsky's *Fantasy for Orchestra* danced around her. Like a sunflower, Laura's head turned towards the music. Her smile returned.

Suddenly, Danny was desperate to say something, to draw her out even more. Yes, she's asleep, but she's *in there*. "Classical music is the best, isn't it? Vaughan Williams, great..." He held up the CD for her, felt stupid, put it back down. "Mussorgsky, he could crank... I love music. I think you can tell a lot about someone by the music they like. I wish you would wake up. There's a lot that we could talk about.

Life must seem like a dream to you... maybe it is a dream? I wonder if you have re-occurring dreams? I do. When I do sleep. I don't sleep a lot. But... I keep dreaming that I'm back at home with my mom and dad, before dad died... and I'm in my bed and everything is cool... then I wake up and I'm here. You don't even know who your parents were. Maybe you're better off where you are."

While he talked, so slowly he barely noticed, Laura took hold of his arm with her hand. Her grip was gentle, but strong, and he had no desire to break it. His eyes traced her arm to her shoulder, her neck then to her face. Laura's eyes were open, filled with wonder.

He met her gaze and lightning struck them both.

Not a literal flash—just something electric that zapped between them, leaping from Laura to Danny.

Somehow, he was eight-years-old again, standing on the landing of the big Mulliner house. There's a little girl with golden hair and big beautiful blue eyes, bathed in golden sunlight, dust motes dancing around her like fairies.

The shock of recognition became an hysterical shout of joy. "I know you!" She smiled back at him, cementing his certainty. "You're that girl! Holy Shit —You're that *girl!*"

Jumping back at the flood of memory: the old dusty house, the little girl on the landing, dropping like a stone in front of him. "All these years … you know I thought I killed you?"

Her big blue eyes are wide now, still wet from her endless sleep, but in them, there was recognition. Slowly, a smile began at the corners of her mouth. She reached for him—the strap around her wrist prevented her touch. Hesitating for just a moment, Danny snapped forward and undid the heavy restraint. The smile widened. Her hand was cool and soft against his cheek and his breath was caught and wouldn't come and *in that minute in that minute in that minute* Danny would do anything to protect her.

Sudden noise broke the spell. Half a dozen men and women in crisp white coats and sharp ties bustled into the room like new owners. Behind them, a tired technicians shoved along heavy and nasty-looking machinery, electro-mechanical monstrosities designed to measure every aspect of verifiable existence. To Danny—and perhaps even to Laura—it was like an invading army.

The leader of the group, wearing his authority and entitlement on his face like the mask of a Greek god, as plain as his manicured beard. Danny vaguely recognized the man's face, and the nametag on the doctor's breast confirmed, the puffed up gentleman was none other than Dr. Bhyle. Dr. Egon Bhyle. He couldn't have dreamed a better villain.

Bhyle and his army breezed past Danny, shunting him aside one-by-one like a bucket brigade. He was a moveable object to their irresistible force. Bhyle had started talking in the hallway and continued his barking. "It seems we've shown up at a propitious time. Our subject is awake. We can take normalized readings for later comparisons."

Only Danny seemed to notice the confused and frightened look on Laura's face. No one else acted concerned.

"You may only have a few minutes, Doctor," said Nurse Evans.

Beside her, Dr. Corso nodded, hoping to assert some level of authority over his own patient. "The durations of her waking state varies from seconds to a little over an hour."

Bhyle didn't respond. He just moved closer to Laura's side while she shrank away from him even further.

Anger was building up inside of Danny, along with alarm that was rapidly evolving into panic. She didn't want that many people around her. Couldn't they tell? Couldn't they see they were freaking her out? *She's only been awake for two minutes, you bastards!* "Excuse me," he demanded. "What's going on?"

Dr. Bhyle stared at Danny, suddenly aware of the man's presence. Like noticing a fly buzzing in a corner. Instead of Danny, Bhyle addressed Dr. Corso, "I understood that she has no relatives."

Laura struggled at her other restraint. Nurse Evans rewrapped the heavy restraint that Danny had undone. Because she'd *wanted* him to!

"He's not a relative," said Dr. Corso, who had no real explanation for who Danny was or what his particular function in the room seemed to be. "He's-"

"Then get him out of here," said Bhyle, turning his back on the room, overseeing the technicians attempt to attach electrodes and wires to Laura's head and chest. She tried to bat them away but the nurse had done a good job at the restraints. "You'll have to leave, young man," said Bhyle to the air. Then to the nurse, his words came out in a hiss: "I thought we talked about this."

Nurse Evans looked mortified, "I was just going to tell him—"

Danny had had enough. "You're scaring her!" But his irrelevance to the situation rendered him invisible.

Bhyle continued to fuss over Laura's chart, this monitor, that one, but never looking at Laura directly. "Is there any reason why we can't move her to the clinic Thursday morning? I want to insulate her from external influences."

"Dr. Bhyle, I do want to point out that you have to be careful with her," said Dr. Corso. "I don't want to have her just wake up in some strange environment."

Invisibility be damned, Danny pointed both hands at Laura, imploring. "She doesn't understand what's going on!"

Meanwhile, Nurse Evans has pulled out an enormous hypodermic needle while Dr. Corso and another orderly begin to hustle invisible Danny out of the room. "We'll take good care of her," said Dr. Corso, without a hint of expression in his voice.

Seeing the needle, Laura's breathing increased. On the verge of hyperventilation, she looked out to Danny, locked eyes with him. He could feel her pain and panic. It overwhelmed his own. Bargaining: "Just give me a second to talk to her."

"You have to leave now," someone said.

Bhyle wouldn't even look in his direction. "Get him out of here. We have to get this
done."

"You have to leave or they're going to call security," said the nurse.

He was no longer invisible—all eyes were on him now. All pleading for him to leave. Except for Laura, whose eyes begged for help. Her mouth opened and closed, but no sound came out.

What could he do? The doctors and nurses had formed a wall between him and Laura's bed. He'd never break such a phalanx. All he could do was lock eyes with Laura and think, real hard, *"I will help you!"*

And maybe… just maybe… she heard him.

The panic in her eyes turned to resignation. Closing her mouth, dropping her hands, she let the nurse and the needle do what they wanted to.

Unable to tear himself from Laura's pain, Danny heard Dr. Corso's voice in his ear. "Son, you really need to go now. She's in good hands. We're going to move her where she'll get some help."

"That's a lie," Danny heard himself mutter. "You're just going to study her like some lab rat."

"I'll get security," he heard someone say. Danny realized this wasn't a battle he could possibly win. "OK, Jesus… I'm going…" he turned and left the room, adding, pathetically, "but don't you hurt her…"

Halfway down the hall, he called back to them, "Don't you hurt her!"

Further down the hall came a little chuckle from Volpe that should have been impossible to hear but it rattled through Danny's head and chased him from the hospital.

Volpe must have enjoyed the whole thing.

CHAPTER 7

Danny needed to do something. Something to help Laura. And he *would* do something, god-damn it.

Soon as he figured out what that something could possibly be.

No work today. No reason to hustle home to the empty apartment. There was a burger joint around the corner from the hospital, *Kewpee's*. There was one of those nightmare-fuel Kewpee Dolls on the sign as a mascot. It was horrifying and suited Danny's mood.

The joint wasn't busy, especially for lunchtime. A few scattered diners, mostly eating alone, in scarred red vinyl booths as far away from each other as possible. Coffee was delivered by one of two waitresses, neither of whom looked like they'd slept since the first Bush was president. *I feel ya, sisters.*

He ordered a burger he didn't want, a soda he wouldn't drink. The coffee he'd downed quickly and asked for a refill. *I have to do something. I have to do something.*

There was a little box of crayons nestled between the salt and paper shakers—those same tan and gray shakers every restaurant in the world has. Red, green, and blue crayons. He pulled out the red, flipped over his placemat and began doodling. Doodling helped him think.

Expose Dr. Bhyle, he thought, crayon scuttling away, *tell the world who he is. Show what he's doing to Laura...*

With a frustrated grunt, he shoved the crayons aside and pulled out his phone to search "Dr. Egon Bhyle."

The very first video to come up was as damning as you could get. "Allegations of abuse and the sudden death of 21-year-old college student Evan Collier have caused local authorities to look deeper into the Bhyle Sleep Study Center run by its controversial head Dr. Egon Bhyle. We spoke with Dr. Bhyle outside of his office at the Center."

Then the video Dr. Bhyle spoke: "I know what you're going to ask me about. The Collier boy... well that was just an unfortunate circumstance."

There he was: that bearded, white-clad example of toxicity. Onscreen, Bhyle continued:

"We had no idea that he had a pre-existing medical condition. It's a sad error... but sometimes these things happen. We have to rely on the applicants to be truthful when they fill out the forms."

The reporter tried to get a word in: "And what about the allegations of abuse?"

Bhyle dismissed the question with an impatient wave of his hand. *I have no time for your bleeding heart attitude...* "We've always treated our research subjects with the greatest of care. This a government-funded facility. There are all sort of checks and balances... and... and you have to understand that nearly all our subjects are paid volunteers..."

"We've been told that sometimes your *experiments* go a little too far."

That word—*experiments*—shot rage sizzling through Danny's skull. He shoved the phone into his pocket.

Pushing away from the table abruptly, Danny overturned his water and empty coffee cup. Liquid splashed and merged into a little tributary on the table, soaking through the crimson crayon portrait of Laura.

CHAPTER 8

UNEXPLAINED SUICIDES at SLEEP CENTER.

Read one headline.
Another one said:

CHARGES OF ABUSE LEVIED AT CON-TROVERSIAL DOCTOR.

Another:

STUDENT DIES AT SLEEP CENTER - OTHER HOSPITALIZED AFTER UN-ORTHODOX EXPERIMENTS.

A-fucking-*nother*:

FURTHER ALLEGATIONS OF SEXUAL ABUSE AT BHYLE SLEEP CENTER.

Danny's speakers played The Plagues, "Why Can't You Be True," a little too loud, but he was in the zone. His days had been filled with hate-re-searching Bhyle, the Sleep Center, and working out The Plan to Do Something for Laura.

It required, so far, a white thrift store lab coat, and Photoshop. From the Bhyle Sleep Clinic website, he found the company logo. Torture with corporate branding. Minutes later, his high quality laser printer spit out a brand new ID tag, Danny's face next to someone named "DR.PETER BURKE – SOMNIOSCOPY."

He'd been in and out of the Hamilton-Hart building with barely ever a glance in his direction. Danny had a strong suspicion that despite the numerous encounters he'd had with Nurse Evans, Dr. Corso, or the security guard—none of them would remember what he looked like. After his last encounter with Bhyle's army in Laura's room, it was clear they considered him a non-entity. He was a background character in a video game that didn't render unless you needed to interact with it. That's exactly what he wanted.

Whenever he needed a break from loathing Dr. Bhyle, he'd research Byron Volpe. It was a toss-up who seemed more evil. The scientist or the serial killer.

As much of a meal the media made of Bhyle's suspected malfeasance, news outlets had created a right banquet out of Volpe's story. After a reign of terror, Volpe's arrest dominated the headlines for months at a time. Since Danny never read the news, it was *all* news to him.

"POLICE DISCOVER MURDER VICTIM AT BOOKSTORE."

ONLY KNOWN PHOTOGRAPH OF BYRON VOLPE:

It was just a blurry, smiling face. The eyes were

black pits. As if the evil in Volpe couldn't be captured by mortal mechanical means. Caption: *Enigmatic rare book dealer. Only known photograph. Bergen County Sheriff's Office 11/27/2002 - #42799*

> *'Byron Volpe Arrested – Wednesday, at the Volpe Bookstore, Byron Volpe, owner, was arrested for his involvement with a series of murders that have gone unexplained until now... channel 9 your news your way.com...'*
> *'Today local officials reported that a body was discovered outside the Volpe Rare Bookstore by a passerby, the Body was stripped of all clothing and lying facedown... Heraldtimes-news.com.'*
> *'Although there is little evidence that he, himself, has committed the murders, he has still managed... see more at USAThisWeek.com'*

Danny could never bring himself to read the articles all the way through. It was clear Volpe was a monster. He'd encountered a bona fide, straight-outta-urban legends, vampiric, mind-controlling monster.

Never any word about Volpe's upbringing, or how he became a "mesmerist and killer." No explanation how he could make seemingly mentally healthy people kill others and then themselves. How he kept his hands clean and mind dirty...

Doesn't matter... thought Danny. *Volpe is irrelevant.*

Bhyle was the real villain. Bhyle was hurting Laura.

Get her away from Bhyle, and she'll be free of Volpe too.

Danny had no idea where that thought came from.

Tomorrow… after work… Danny intended to do something.

ONCE UPON A TIME, there was a sad little boy named Byron who didn't like being told what to do.

Not by parents. Not by teachers. Not by the other kids in the yard.

Byron's family had a neighbor, Jerome. He lived in the same run-down apartment building, just down the hall. Nobody liked to visit this neighbor. His parents told Byron to stay away from the neighbor, which only made him want to meet him all the more.

It took some time to gain Jerome's trust. Jerome wanted do things to Byron that he was too little to understand. He never got a chance because Byron knew the neighbor's secrets and was becoming aware that he had a subtle power over people. A power, a glance, and that strange tone that he had in his voice. Byron's black soul had a power and he knew it.

Jerome had stacks of old books. Books on the Occult, books on the Supernatural. Books that taught you how to get others to do what you wanted. Little Byron learned fast. That's how he got mom and dad to burn down the apartment building with everyone in it. Just a few suggestions, the words in the right order. He learned how to make the worms come out.

Byron sat and watched as Mommy and Daddy waved to him from the window even as they burned to death. Byron sat digging a little grave in the yard for a small bird that had "suddenly died." He was adding it to the little cemetery he had been working on for months. He watched the flames engulf the building as he listened to the sound Jerome screaming and pounding on the locked door to his apartment. Suddenly Jerome found the door open. He ran out screaming. Byron smiled as he watched him running out of the building in to the arms of the Police. "Someone" had apparently told the authorities that Jerome had set fire to the building.

Obviously, it was best for all involved.

People in big yellow suits zipped all the blackened corpses into even blacker bags. Little Byron found the charred skeletons fascinating. Like they'd been yanked out of a barbecue, flesh falling off the bone. He couldn't tell one from another. Who had been Mrs. Spencer? Which ones were mommy and daddy?

When Jerome returned, after the cops let him go again, he saw the smoldering lot where his home used to be. The Byron sat surrounded by Jerome's rescued books. Jerome now knew the full power of Little Byron and it terrified him to the core. Jerome would now do whatever Little Byron asked.

Little Byron no longer had to go to school. He no longer had the desire to play ball or run or jump or shout. He liked telling people what to do and watching them do it.

"The sign says 'Walk'," he once told a man in a suit.

He was a grown up, so he waved the little boy away.

"I can see that!" he said. The bus bounced him so high into the air. Like someone had thrown a sock monkey.

When he got a little older, Byron, still scrawny and still angry, learned a new word, and it described the neighbor. So he made the worms come out.

For hours, he watched Jerome slowly remove

strips of skin from his arms and legs with an old straight razor, crying with every long, long cut. The little boy had learned a new word: flensing. The neighbor cried so hard as he applied the table salt to his wounds, straight from the can with the little girl and her umbrella on the label.

The neighbor bawled and wept and begged. "Why am I doing this, Byron? Make me stop!"

Jerome screamed and cried and apologized and said he couldn't help it. Tears still flowed from the neighbor's eyes, even after he'd thumbed the sockets clean.

When his tongue went, the neighbor could only moan as he slashed at the bottoms of his bare feet, and made a worse fuss when the little boy made him hop, hard, over to the window. He made the neighbor *want* to put his head through the glass and rub his face against the remaining shard. He made the neighbor *want nothing more* than to crawl out of that window and leap out.

Little Byron made the neighbor crawl back up the three flights of stairs, on broken hands and legs, in order to jump again. He made him *want to.*

Over time, little Byron grew. Faster than he'd imagined, he became a big man. A hulking, imposing, powerful man. He never, ever had to use his size or strength to get people to do what he wanted. It was all in the mind.

Everyone was a marionette at heart. A plaything, and Byron Volpe was the only one who could see the strings.

CHAPTER 9

When Billy Dornboss entered his revolving door of rehab stints, he brought with it a new running joke. He'd ring Danny at odd hours—7:25 AM, 9:03 PM—and say, "I need tacos, break me out of here."

"You're not incarcerated," Danny would say. "Sign yourself out and go get tacos."

"No, you gotta bust me out of here! Now. I stuck a matchbook in the back door and the nurses change shift at…"

Sometimes Danny would indulge him. He'd park in the back, keep the motor running while Billy dove out a clearly-marked door and barrel-rolled to the car. Then he'd rattle off the shift changes, where the camera blind spots were, which doors had alarms and which doors just had alarm signs. "You're one messed up prescription away from getting the blueprints tattooed on your chest," Danny said.

"You know how expensive it is to get a tattoo in invisible UV ink? I have to save up."

For all his paranoia, not to mention his desperate need for attention, Billy Dornboss had an obsessive mind for minutiae and detail. Armed with this knowledge, Danny drove to the Hamilton Hospital with only the vaguest TV-plot of a plan. Doing Something suddenly seemed inadequate.

Keeping his head down, he was happy to see that the hospital was in the midst of its afternoon activity. The waiting area was busy, the admin ladies looked hassled and annoyed. Perfect.

He had all his supplies in a bag slung over his shoulder, but he didn't feel like Ethan Hunt. He felt like one of the lesser Muppets. As casually as he could seem without whistling, he ducked into the men's room and unpacked his "disguise." White shirt, black tie, white lab coat, fake ID. No longer Danny Sloan. He was now "Dr. Peter Burke – Somnioscopy." Whatever the hell *that* was.

Now that he was in costume Danny realized he actually had to *play* the part. He'd included a clipboard in his bag of props. Even cursory inspection would see that the page on top was his phone bill, but he kept his head down as he walked, thrift store shoes clacking and squeaking down the hall, screaming to others that he was an *infiltrator*!

Heart pounding hard enough his lungs felt battered, Danny tried to project the attitude of "Doctor." From his observation, it was an attitude comprised of a heavy stew of arrogance, entitlement, trust fund money, and Generic White Man Syndrome. At least the latter would come easy. For the rest… he'd have to hope his natural ability to fade into any background would finally work in his favor.

A pair of nurses in green scrubs angled by him without a look in his direction. Not at his face. Not at his ID. It was official. He didn't exist. Danny allowed himself to exhale.

Passing a big, beefy orderly he'd seen on the

floor in the past, neither man acknowledged the other. Instead, Danny pivoted down a narrow hallway and grabbed the nearest wheel chair from a bank parked along the wall. He tried to just keep going—*casual walking, I'm supposed to be here*—but almost immediately hit a dead end. Hanging an awkward U-turn, Danny hustled back the way he came and headed towards Laura's room.

IN THE DARK PADDED ROOM, the room without a number, the only room on the floor with a re-enforced steel door with double-locks, the "patient" was losing his mind.

Bam! Bam! Bam! Byron Volpe bashed his head against the padded wall. The pain was nothing compared to his rage. Beneath the hood, his jaw worked and chewed and thrashed against the hateful medieval gag they'd forced into his mouth. When he wanted it to be, Volpe's tongue could be a fist. With an animalistic grunt, he forced the fucking thing out and screamed to the ceiling, "He's here! He's going to take her! She's *mine!*"

Once upon a time, Byron Volpe had been a sad, angry, *weak* little boy, who learned to use his mind to hurt people. He grew up. He was no longer a *weak* little boy. Nor was he sad. Angry, he remained. A guttural snarl escaped his throat as he flexed his biceps and strained against his restraints. Any other man (hung 24-hours a day, suspended from straps held to the walls, never allowed a sitting position, denied all movement and much of his senses, always in the dark, without companionship, entertainment, *light)* would have found his strength wanting.

At the end of the snarl, he'd pulled his right arm

free. The strap snapped from the wall like a severed tendon.

AN ALARM WENT OFF, emanating from nowhere, but filling every corner. "Dr. Peter Burke" froze where he stood, hands gripping the wheelchair handles, sweat trickling through white knuckles. Orderlies, nurses, security guards rushed down the hall behind him, closing in on him quick. Danny closed his eyes against the inevitable, waiting for the slam against the wall, the twisted wrists, the strangling hand-cuffs—

The panicked crew rushed past him and continued down the hall. He was still invisible! Wasting no time, he steered the wheelchair into Laura's room where the sleeping princess lay beneath snaking tubes and wires.

Even breathing seemed like inviting disaster. Undoing the straps at her wrists and ankles was easy. It took a few seconds to understand how to detach her body from the machines. There were sticky pads for the electrodes and he was terrified he'd taken off a layer of her smooth skin peeling them away. Thank god there was no catheter. There *was* the feeding tube snaked into her nose.

Crash! Bang! The commotion down the hall continued. Running footsteps. People shouting. Over it all, he could hear Volpe howling. Hands shaking, Danny tugged at the feeding tube. And tugged. It came out of her nostril an inch at a time. And it kept on coming. Like a reverse tapeworm. Still sleeping, Laura winced in pain. Danny pulled his hands back.

"I'm sorry. I'm sorry," he whisper-spoke. A

quick glance at the open door showed him all attention remained on Volpe—who screamed:

"He's here, you idiots! She's mine! He's taking her!"

Returning to the task, Danny took a deep breath and didn't let it out until the end of the tube came free from Laura's nostril. No blood. She coughed a little but remained asleep. "Okay… okay…" That became Danny's mantra.

Finally free of her bonds, the princess still slumbered as he lifted her from bed. She weighed even less than he'd expected and he got her easily into the chair. Her head fell back and Laura whimpered.

"No-no-no," Danny said. "Don't wake up. I have to get you out of here." He tucked a blanket around her and wheeled her towards the door, whisper-singing, *"Sweet dreams are made of these… who am I to disagree…"* as he watched her eyes close again. He sighed again. "Okay…"

Danny stood.

The big security guard filled the doorway.

In surprise, with a soupçon of panic, Danny grinned wide and said, "Hiiiii." Really loud. Too loud.

Another crash from the hallway. The security guard craned his neck into Laura's room, then back to the commotion.

Then back to Danny. "Who are you?" the guard demanded. Big handsome black security guard. Not one of those doughy retired cops. This guy was out of central casting as "Hero."

I am ever so fucked, thought Danny. "I'm… uh…" (*Jesus fucking Christ, who the fuck am I??*) He held up his now-extremely obviously-homemade ID badge. "Dr. Peter…*mmrrrrmr,*" Danny said, unable to read his alias upside-down.

Another smash and howl from the corridor. *Please be distracted. Please go be a hero over there.*

Danny kept up his demented grin. Laura's head tilted back. She snored at him. "Oh, yeah—I'm from the... ah Bhyle Center for Sleep Studies..." He held up his ID again. "See?"

Another crash from the hallway, but this time the guard didn't budge. Because of course not. Danny continued his verbal tap-dance. The key to a good lie is in the details, right? This is why he'd never tried to break Billy out. "I'm here to transfer this patient in room 1169..." He pulled a slip of paper from his pocket, hoping that the guard didn't see it was a drug store receipt. "...a... Laura Baxter... To the center." He pointed to the top of Laura's head. "Laura Baxter, right? And this is room 1169, right?"

The guard stared at him. Pointed a finger at the number on the door: 1169. "Yeah," said the guard, not budging. "Everything OK?"

"Where?" said Danny. Then his terrified brain kicked him. "Oh, yeah. In here? No. Here? No, but... I heard a little commotion going on down the hall."

Another crash indicated the commotion was in progress.

"Guy in the rubber room next door got a little frisky, thought someone was stealing his girlfriend. You're lucky he didn't get loose."

Somebody down the hall shouted in pain. Danny looked at the guard. "Yeah," he said.

Volpe was screaming, over and over, *"She's mine! She's mine!"*

Danny made a final attempt. He summoned all of his male entitlement and said to the guard, the Black guard, "We all good here?"

While the guard didn't care for the tone, it was at least a tone he was familiar with. Dismissive authority, even from a little punk in a white coat. The guard fixed him with a hard stare, then moved aside. "You have a good night," he said. Then another crash from the hallway, another shout from Volpe, and the guard decided to join in the fun.

Finally, the coast, as it were, seemed clear.

Dr. Peter Mrmrmr wheeled patient Laura Baxter as quickly and casually as possible towards the Emergency Exit.

It wasn't until he had her bundled into the front seat, belted in, secure and wrapped in the blanket and his civvie jacket, that he realized he'd been holding his breath the entire time. Letting it out, spots danced before his eyes for a time, mocking him in the glow of the sodium street lamps above. When his vision cleared, reality sank in. The jailbreak wasn't over.

Once they'd left the parking structure and reached the ramp for the highway, Danny was certain they weren't being followed. No one was after them. They were...

Beside him, Laura snored softly.

...*free?*

IT TOOK four orderlies to wrestle Volpe back into his straps. And that was only after he was injected with tranquilizers and Thorazine. And that only happened after the four orderlies and *six* security guards had gotten him to the ground and sat on him.

And *that* only happened after Volpe had broken two men's noses, and one woman's jaw.

All the while screaming *"She's mine! She's mine!"*

Finally—*finally*—he was back in his crucifixion suit, straps re-enforced, double-bolted to the wall, hanging from his arms like scarecrow or a puppet.

Out of spite, they left the blood on the walls. Give him *something* to look at the next time he got his hood off.

Barely conscious, gagged, limp, Volpe continued to make a steady noise, almost a snore. If it were intelligible, it would have been understood as "Tick-tock, tick-tock…"

CHAPTER 10

HE'D PULLED IT OFF. IT HAD GONE BETTER THAN HE could have dreamed.

Danny held his breath every time they passed anything that looked like a cop car—*undercovers use Lincoln Town-cars, right? Would they drive a green one?*—but it was as if they'd escaped an entirely different reality.

Exiting the highway, a light rain began to fall, the spatters on the windshield refracting the light, splashing shadow across Laura's peaceful face. Danny flipped on the wipers, and the shadows danced away. He looked at her and couldn't help but smile.

It was like she heard the smile. As if on cue, Laura's eyelids fluttered open. For an instant they took him in, and a smile of her own began to form.

On the other side of the road, a car bellowed an angry honk at some perceived aggression and the blood drained from Laura's face. Her eyes went wide.

It felt like falling. In Lauraland, she could fly. Only in the Ash Land did she fall. But not like this —not falling forward so fast in a glass cage while everything came at her with lights and noise and so much noise and where was she and what is happening— *whatishappeningwhatishappening?* —

Laura screamed pure primal terror. It scared the shit out of Danny and he jerked the wheel to the right, the lizard part of his brain suddenly interpreting oncoming traffic as danger. The car fishtailed—Laura screamed again—Danny fought the wheel and the car to regain control.

"What?" Danny screamed back, all adrenaline. "What is it?"

Unable to find the words, Laura could only move her hands, motioning that things were coming towards her. Still, Danny's brain was debating flight or fight and he couldn't understand. "What?" he struggled to understand. "Fingers... moving...? Things... Things hitting you?—*Shit.*" It finally hit him. "The car... You've never been driving?" The relief washed over him. "You've never been driving. Of course. You've never... sure, why would you have?"

Reaching out, Laura slapped at the windshield. "Out!" she demanded.

Danny nodded, pleased he was beginning to understand her. "You want to get out."

She stared at him hard and pointed, "*Ouuutt!*" Again, she slapped the windshield, then began banging on her side window.

"Stop," Danny said, looking for a place to pull over. "Don't do that. You're gonna break the glass. OK.... Take it easy. I'll let you out."

There was a little park up ahead and Danny eased the car to the curb. Parking quickly, he hurried out to the other side before Laura could slap the window out. He threw the door open and she followed, spilling onto the grass.

Danny felt his ego slide from triumphant to helpless without warning. He could only watch as Laura pressed her face to the damp grass. Not too far from them, an older couple stared at them. A little old man held the hand of a little old lady who held a leash of a little old dog. All three gaped at them.

He reached down for Laura but she scrabbled away. Forcing a smile for the old people's benefit, Danny tried again to snag her shoulder. "Sweetheart... You probably don't want to do that. You're showing your underwear, babe."

A *squeak*. Danny jumped. So did the little dog. Proud and playful, Laura rolled over, a rubber newspaper in her mouth. She bit down and it squeaked again. The little dog let out a jealous bark.

"Laura, you don't know where that's..." He grabbed the toy and she bit down harder, fighting him.

She knew this game from Lauraland. "Doggy." And now she had someone real to play with!

But Danny didn't understand the game. His heart was pounding. Any second now, the old couple was going to call the cops and the whole plan would be ruined. "She's into nature... Grew up in New York... didn't see much grass there... Except for Central Park—Honey, let's get in the car —no, don't eat that!"

He fished a Twinkie wrapper from her hand. She fought against getting to her feet, giggling.

This wasn't Lauraland. This wasn't Hospital. Where was this? So cool and soft and hard and sweet? Smells that didn't burn or make her sick. And feels. All the things that touched back... There weren't a lot of smells in Lauraland. Only what Hospital snuck in. Everything here smelled so... so... Was this what 'dreaming' was like? She couldn't help but look up at her Fairy Prince and smile, smile so big and wide.

The Sleepiness was coming over her again. She hoped when she woke up, she'd still be in this new *somewhere*.

"She does this a lot," she heard Danny say. "It's fun." Then this new *outside* spun away from her and the nothingness took over and she fell and fell until she didn't know anymore...

Laura's eyes rolled up and her body went limp and she slid right out of Danny's arms, landing face-first again on the grass. Still keeping an eye on the couple, Danny scooped her up again. "She's... very tired. Rough day..."

But the couple only watched. They watched as the weird young man pack the drunk coed into his car. Later, they would wonder if he was a good Samaritan, or one of the usual bad ones. They watched him drive off. Finally, the little old man turned to the little old woman and pointed at the little old dog, "I told you to leave Clancy's toys at home."

ONCE THE PARK was blocks behind, Danny allowed himself to relax again. It wasn't that late but the traffic was sparse nonetheless. Even the lights seemed to be in his favor. *Good. Just let us get home.*

Though Laura was safely unconscious, Danny kept to the speed limit. He didn't want her to wake up and freak out again.

The instant the thought was finished, Laura's eyes fluttered again. Like she could hear his thoughts stirring her back to the waking world. Before her terror could take root again, Danny reached out and touched her arm, anticipating the need.

"It's okay," he said, feeling like the Knight Protector. "Nothing's going to hurt you." ("*Not while I'm around,*" Angela Lansbury sang in his head.)

Laura nodded. She didn't have the words to tell him she understood, so she parroted back. "It's okay. Nothing's going to hurt you... Like..." She found the word! "Fun?"

Danny smiled back at her with an odd sense of pride. "Yeah..." he reached out and picked a small clump of grass from her cheek. "Fun."

Like a cat, Laura rubbed against his fingers. Then her face fell into sadness. "We going to... Hospital?"

In the passing lights and abstract shadows, Laura's face glowed with a beautiful innocence. Danny felt overcome just then, empathy swelling his chest and clumping his throat.

Finally, he managed to cough out a response, "No... we're going *home.*"

She knew that word. "Home?" *Home was Lauraland. How could they drive there?*

Maybe he saw the question on her face, or maybe he could "hear" her thoughts too. "We're going to my home... to where I live. Is that... is that OK?"

She beamed. She nodded hard. "OK."

Her smile changed then into something puzzling. Danny heard liquid running. Laura heard it too. Looking down, she realized she'd wet herself. But the darkness and the nothing was coming again. Before she could apologize, sleep took over.

Danny sighed. They'd both had a big day and they were so close to home.

IN HIS RAGE, Volpe had ripped the straps clear from their quad-bolted security latches in the ceiling. He'd managed to chew his specially-made gag into uselessness. It had taken an inhuman amount of sedation cocktail to bring him down to the ground. Even then, it had taken the biggest orderlies they had to wrestle the maniac into a straightjacket. Over this, they placed *another* straightjacket.

No one argued that the hood on his head restricted his breathing, much less the rag stuffed into his mouth and held there with a heavy Velcro strap. *Please*, let the motherfucker suffocate.

Or let him bash his fucking brains out against the padded walls. With his legs secured, he thrashed on the floor like a giant, enraged maggot. Squirming and writhing in his bonds.

Nobody cared if this didn't look a lick like "rehabilitation." Nobody wanted the monster anywhere near them. "Why the fuck doesn't this state have the death penalty?" one of the orderlies grumbled. Nobody answered.

Constrained but not immobilized, Volpe kicked and rolled, slammed his head and feet against the floor. Through his layers of constriction, he shouted over and over some muffled atrocity no one could quite make out, but they didn't have to. It was his psycho mantra again: "TICK...TICK...TICK..." Coming out "Gugg...Gugg...Gugg..." which made it all the worse.

No matter where you were in the ward, you could hear the psycho maggot. It was like he was in your head. In *everybody's* head.

Not even Dr. Corso was immune. Advil mingled with the caffeine but neither paid attention to his throbbing headache. He tried not to focus on Volpe. Volpe wasn't even his patient, for Christ's sake, and the hulking brute made the good doctor question his Hippocratic Oath. *Can I do harm second?*

He had bigger problems. Laura Baxter was gone. Someone was to blame, even though Corso wasn't that kind of guy. But it sure as hell wasn't *his* fault. "I don't understand how this could happen," he said helplessly. "She was strapped down." But he knew what the nurse was going to say next.

Nurse Evans was already on the defense. It wasn't *her* fault either. "She may have awoken, worked the straps loose. She's done it before…"

Corso said that last bit in his head with her. *She's done it before.* But Laura never made it far before being discovered sound asleep in another room or supply closet or chapel or… she *always* turned up.

The throbbing headache took on a persona. A tall skinny kid he'd constantly caught in her room. "Or maybe somebody let her go." Then he thought, but didn't say, *Or took her with him.*

Nurse Evans was unmoved. "Well she can't get far, and she'll just go back to sleep."

Normally, Dr. Corso practiced patience with his staff. He'd grown up privileged, but he was sure as hell not one of *those* kinds of guys. He understood not every one had had his advantages. Just the same, between the headache and the stress of the missing patient, the last thing he wanted to do was to explain, yet again, the particular nature of Laura Baxter's malady.

"You haven't read her charts carefully, Ms. Evans," he hissed through his teeth. Later, he'd regret this exchange, but the mood was already set. "Ms. Baxter is a somnambulist. That means she's a sleepwalker." The nurse started to argue against his condescension, but he powered through. "She can carry out very complicated actions completely asleep. Sometimes these complicated actions can be *dangerous*. To herself, to others. Look—just have security search the grounds. If they don't find her we'll call the police."

They parted ways then. Corso realized suddenly that he had to go in the same direction as Nurse Evans, but his shamed ego wouldn't let him proceed. He'd just have to walk around. Which would take him, again, past Volpe's "rehabilitation dungeon."

Behind the specially reinforced door, Volpe banged and shouted and thumped and was positively ceaseless. One of those patients that never seem to tire themselves out. Still, Corso couldn't remember a time when the giant was this agitated for this long. "*She's mine*," Corso remembered Volpe saying. He'd never stopped to ask "She who?"

In truth, he just didn't want to know.

The corridor split just after Volpe's door. Dr. Corso kept his head down, made the sharp left. Then it felt like something grabbed him—he couldn't explain it further. Something invisible held the back of his neck and tried to drag him to Volpe's door. He fought the urge to open the door— *no...* he fought the urge *to want to open the door.* He knew he didn't want to, yet there was something now telling him that opening the door was the best and most honorable thing he could ever do.

Dr. Corso actually halted in his stride. He felt himself turn towards the door. He saw his hand reaching for the security pad. He...

It hurt to turn back. It hurt to shake his head to rid these intrusive thoughts and wants. Resuming his walk, his headache became an angry living thing, clawing at his brain, slashing and chewing at his skull.

Reaching his office, Dr. Corso sank down hard into his chair and put his head in his hands. Far, far back in his mind, nagging like Jiminy Cricket, was a tiny voice insisting that he should still—

Stand up.

Go Back.

Open. The. Door.

CHAPTER 11

Miraculously, nobody saw Danny carrying a small, mostly-naked unconscious blonde girl out of the elevator and into his apartment. The last thing he needed was to run into Sara or one of the other neighbors who had an uncanny ability to sense when he was coming and going.

It took some shuffling—Laura wasn't heavy, but he really should have gotten his keys ready before carrying her—before he finally got them both through the door and into the relative safety of his apartment. And once the door was closed, he realized he had nowhere to put her down. In all this time, he still hadn't gotten around to bringing his record collection to order. Vinyl was stacked everywhere. On the table, on the couch, both chairs, the bathtub.

He almost dropped her while struggling to clear a path on the carpet with his feet. It pained him to kick aside the wax—there goes *The White Album* right under the couch. Finally, he'd blazed enough of a path for Laura to stretch out on the floor. Her face and hands were smeared with grass and dirt, and quite frankly, she had a hospital funk to her that even *she* had to be sick of by now.

Grabbing a pillow from his bed, he slid it under her head to make her more comfortable. Then he filled a dish tub with warm soapy water, grabbed some towels, brought them to her side. As he started to remove her gown, reality hit him like a slap. Uncovered, completely naked, Laura was a vision. She'd been well taken care of. Suddenly, Danny felt unworthy to look at her, much less touch her—much less *bathe* her. It felt almost sacrilegious. On his floor, between the jazz and the Creedence, was a nude angel.

Dipping the sponge into the warm water, Danny moved it along her arms and legs. It was tender. Nothing about this felt sexual. For a brief moment, he thought of medieval maidens whose job it was to bathe corpses prior to burial. For another brief moment, he thought of archaeologists gently cleaning statues of flawless marble. She was like a fine painting, classical, Pre-Raphaelite, her beauty, crippling. There was a tragic aura to her face that made him want to protect her.

There was no plan. He didn't know what the fuck he was doing. He just knew he was doing the right thing. Admittedly, in the wrongest possible way.

Just then, Laura's eyes opened with that delicate flutter Danny had to admit he'd fallen in love with. She gazed up at him with intense blue eyes. Then following his gaze to his hands. His hands on her body. Suddenly, Danny felt ashamed. He pulled back just a little, but she smiled. She touched his hands, letting him know it was okay. Then, again, she was asleep.

Because she was safe.

Or, at least, that's what Danny hoped.

Denise had left nothing of her own behind. There wasn't a scrap of memory to be found, let alone any abandoned clothing. Danny gathered up some of his own clothes—t-shirts, hoodies, sweatpants, whatever was clean. Shoes would be an issue. He stared down at the canoes at the ends of his legs. Maybe if they stuffed an extra pair of socks in the toes?

At first, he wasn't sure if he should try to help dress her but Laura managed well enough. The sneakers were slip-on, so there was no awkward lace-tying. Laura held her arms out from her sides, as if looking for approval, with the biggest smile on her face, happiness meeting her eyes. Danny had no choice but to smile back. His voice caught in his throat and he could only manage a thumbs-up.

They took the rear staircase down—he thought the elevator might be too overwhelming for someone who just grasped the concept of driving. "I'm glad you woke up," he said. "I want to show you a lot of cool stuff."

"Cool stuff," she echoed, with a nod and a smile.

Down the sidewalk and through the creaky metal gate, Danny guided her into the Outside. It was late, but it wasn't *super late*. Stores would still be open in the gentrified district around the corner. Still, the street was relatively quiet and the moon was full.

Laura's eyes were wide as she took it all in. "Moon," she said, pointing. "Cool stuff!"

Danny took her hand. "I know, let's just walk..."

Her fingers over his lips almost stopped the

words. The touch was gentle but curious, like she was feeling for his voice. "Let's... let's just walk," she said, and beamed as if a decision had been reached.

Danny's smile came automatically. It was like watching a visitor from another planet—or maybe another realm. Again, he thought of an angel who hadn't been to earth in a long, long time. So he said the first dumb thing to come into his head: "Do you want to get some ice cream?"

Laura nodded. She knew the words. "Do you want to get some..."

"No, look, that was a question. You say... 'Yes, I want some ice cream'."

Understanding lit up her eyes. She stood tall, shoulders back. "Yes, I want some ice cream..." Then added, "Please."

He cocked his head at her. "Are you messing with me?"

But all she did was mimic his movement.

TEN MINUTES and a few blocks later, they reached the ice cream shop. A minute or so more, and Danny had ice cream cones to deliver. He chose one of the iron patio seats outside and passed Laura the flavor she'd chosen: strawberry.

He was more of a Moose Tracks fan.

Laura stared at her treat, felt along the ridges of the cone. Her finger came to the soft cold part and her face lit up again. Danny watched her with as much wonder as she felt for the cone.

(If Danny really could hear her thoughts, perhaps he'd know that there was all kinds of ice cream in Lauraland, but it never had much of a taste, and it never felt cold. In Lauraland, you can't really *feel* things. Just the *memory* of how things felt. In Lauraland, this ice cream would have tasted, and felt… pink. This oozing over her fingers was *so* different… sweet…)

"Cold," she said, not tasting, just watching as the ice cream tilted precariously.

Danny reached forward, "Wait, it's gonna fall."

With an audible "plop," the sloppy scoop hit the chrome tabletop. Danny hated to think of the parade of grimy fingers that had already touched the surface. But he stopped worrying. Laura wasn't eating the treat. Instead, she used it as a medium to paint the table. Then, like an ancient shaman (or perhaps a two-year-old) she smeared it across her face and beamed at him through the pink mess.

There were no witnesses on the street, so Danny let himself laugh. "I just got you cleaned up. Now, I'm going to have to give you another bath." Instantly, he felt like a pervert. "I mean… um… I'm gonna get some napkins."

As he stood, Laura's eyes closed and she slowly slid from her chair and under the table.

His cone in one hand, the other gesturing helplessly, Danny finally shrugged. "Okay, then."

The errant knight disposed the decadent desserts into the trash and then saw his maiden home.

AT THE HOSPITAL, outside Laura Baxter's room, stood three men and none of them looked like they wanted to be there. All three were tired, hands jittery from too much coffee, stomachs seizing for the same reason. First, there was the eternally beleaguered Dr. Corso, standing in his shirt and tie, jacket long abandoned. The other two wore cheap, rumpled suits, and did so proudly. It was their uniform.

Detective Garrett had the skin of an old leather sofa. His face had reached his 50s long before linear time caught up. His hair was thinning and he wore it slicked back and resentful.

The other detective-Conroy-still had a full head of hair. Conroy was probably born a detective, likely in the same ugly raincoat. Probably the same age as Conroy but still somehow much older. He walked with the gait of a bowling pin as he came away from the porthole in Volpe's room and joined them.

"I was hoping you might remember something more about this art student guy," said Garrett.

Dr. Corso shook his head, repeating what was becoming his mantra. "He just seemed like a good kid…"

"I think that's a quote from Hitler's mom," said Conroy.

"Any idea where he lives?" Garrett asked him.

The back and forth was doing nothing for Corso's headache. "No. You should ask the main desk."

"We did," said Garrett. He had a slow, deep voice, some might refer to as 'oafish.' "Signed in as 'Van Decker.' The name and number both phony."

"Van Decker played guitar for The Plagues," said Conroy. His voice was reedier, and it had a tone that suggested everything was a joke with a lousy punch line.

Garrett took the bait. "How the fuck do you know?"

"I'm multi-layered," said Conroy. "What's up with that Volpe character?"

Corso mumbled to his shoes, "Delusional, Psychopathic, Sociopathic… Bad guy."

"What's he mumbling?"

"The only thing he really ever says," said Corso. "'Tick, tick, tick…' he just says it over and over."

"What is he, a fucking clock?" asked Conroy. "You couldn't get some nice patient who just thinks he's Napoleon?"

"And what's with the canvas burrito you got him wrapped up in? That part of his therapy?"

Corso sighed, "He's convinced that the missing girl, Laura Baxter, belongs to him."

"Belongs to him?" said Conroy, though it wasn't a question. "Sick fuck."

"Dangerous fuck," said Corso, too tired to police his own language. "He fractured both legs and broke the nose of one of our attendants trying to get loose. Then he tried to push the man's broken nose up into his brain… nearly killed him. This seems to be the best arrangement for Mr. Volpe right now."

Suddenly, Conway was a lot more interested. "Volpe? Byron Volpe? That's Byron Volpe you have in there?"

"Most soulless person I've ever met."

Again, Garrett chimed in. "I know about this case. Hypnotist or something."

"Uncanny ability with it."

Garrett nodded. "Hypnosis is bullshit."

"Yeah?" said Conroy. "Tell that to his wife. She died trying to get away from his hold over her. Who knows how many people this scuzzball has killed? I was *on* that case. We never found all the bodies, just the one he wanted us to find." A humorless smile spread across the man's face. It was at home there. "Just the ones that looked like suicide. And, fuck you, hypnosis helped my second wife quit smoking."

Maybe it was the eighth cup of coffee kicking in, or maybe it was a desperate move to end the conversation, but Dr. Corso's brain conjured something actually useful. "A moment, Detective, I just remembered something." Now he had the albeit skeptical attention of both men. "I think the kid might have been a friend of someone we had in here for court-ordered drug rehab. A tweaker named Dornboss. Used to steal all the locks off the doors, polish all the little brass parts then put them back. We can check the records?"

The detectives nodded. Garrett took another second to peer back into Volpe's room. "Dornboss?" he muttered idly, then followed the other two men down the hall.

No one heard Volpe say, "Dornboss... Dornboss... Tick, tick, tick, Dornboss..."

CHAPTER 12

After the long day, Danny collapsed onto his couch and slept the dreamless sleep of the dead.

Tucked into Danny's bed, Laura felt happy and safe in Danny's world. She drifted away to her land of sunlight and shade.

Until she was ripped away from *Lauraland*.

The grass at her feet turned to ash. The ash rose and choked out the sun. The world around her went black and gray and hard and sharp. Beneath her feet, the ground shook and threatened to topple her. Then she heard the thunderous roar of earth cracking and rock screaming. About her, new mountains were born, stabbing up at the iron sky.

Laura wanted to run, but the landscape became a maze, lined by giant skeletons the size of lighthouses, draped in rotting robes, empty sockets like train tunnels glaring down at her, spilling their darkness over her like oil, soiling her beautiful white dress, corrupting the material, slicking her skin like an unwanted touch.

Some of the skeletal giants had lost their heads. The boulder skulls her height and bigger judging her as she tried to speed past them. Her legs didn't want to work. The air was so thick around them, fighting against movement.

This is not my world!

Another horrific scream from the earth and out spit a graveyard of coffins, jutting out at odd angles like rotting teeth. Lids lurched open, revealing the shuddering things inside. Like bodies that had been skinned and sewn back on inside out. They had dead eyes. Many of the coffins were empty, the contents having long rotted away. Or eaten by their tortured neighbors.

There is no color. No light. No hope.

Laura screamed up at the giant skeletal judges: *I don't belong here*!

But she heard the skittering, slithering, clattering behind her. Vomitus creatures coming to touch her. With no choice but to run through the graveyard of empty coffins, Laura trudged through the ash, moving in slow motion, the jagged ground beneath her feet tearing at the tender soles. She ran. And ran. Into the maze of revolving black mirrors.

The things were still behind her. Or maybe just *one thing* with millions of legs. A mirror before her stopped revolving, showing her clearly: tired, smeared, frightened beyond reason. She could *feel* here. Pain. Her chest hurt from the ash and thick air. The wind whipped at her thin dress and exposed skin, cold and sharp.

"Let me dream!" she screamed to the sky, to the world without a horizon. "Please let me dream! Take me away to that other place! I want the dream *with Danny!*"

The mirror before her spun with such ferocity she had to jump back. It flipped once, like a card revealed in a magic trick, but she wasn't alone in the reflection. Something behind her wrapped its invisible arms around her and, in the reflection, *be-*

came her. A new face grew over her own—teeth bared, smiling without humor, black eyes without love, burning flames inside black tunnels. The whipping wind around her formed the rest of the head.

"*Laura...*" said the voice. The voice belonged to Byron Volpe, a name she'd never heard before but knew him intimately and in ways she didn't want to ever understand. "*You are my blood...*" the face said around her own, like it was chewing her head. The voice caressed the inside of her skull and left behind slime. "*I am you. You have nothing to fear from me. It's is the Clouded Man who stalks you.*"

Ringing, clanging, vibrating violently against the vicious wind, the mirror plates around her twisted and spun, each reflecting the face of Volpe and Volpe alone. The shadow engulfed her image, then reacheed out for her. As it sucked away the last of the light, the mirror turned to rust.

Something even worse was behind her now. It was faster than her. It would wear her skin well.

Danny had carried Laura into what constituted his living room, got her bundled on the couch, TV on, TV table in front of her. She'd vaguely woken once as he filled the bowl, then her eyes fluttered closed again. "You have to wake up," he said. "I don't have a feeding tube."

The clock was ticking. He had to get to work.

Desperate, he shoved a spoon of soggy Cheerios into her mouth and tried to manipulate her jaw into chewing. Then she woke up, and fixed him with the most vicious "*What the fuck?*" look he'd ever seen. She slapped his hand away.

"Not a baby!" She took the spoon from him to prove it, but was asleep again before she could reach the bowl.

Danny realized then he sucked at planning. All the thought he'd put into liberating the sleeping princess... what the hell were the next steps to "happily ever after"?

He mumbled some instructions to the sleeping Laura. "If you get hungry you can just help yourself. I have to go now. Please don't touch anything or go anywhere..." Every corner in the room seemed to be sharp and dangerous and there was absolutely nothing he could do about it now. "Yeah, OK..."

The hallway was empty when Danny stepped out, but by the time he'd gotten the door locked, it wasn't. As he turned, High-Maintenance Sara bopped out of the elevator, dry cleaning bag over her shoulder. He tried to be invisible.

"Danny!" she sang to him off key. "How are you?"

He froze. Maybe her vision was based on movement. Like a velociraptor. No such luck. "Morning, Sara."

Sara attempted a casual lean against the wall, but was just far enough away that she almost bounced. With a quick clear of her throat to cover, she said, "Hey, did I see you come in with a rather, uh, good-looking girl last night?" She smiled like a bear trap.

No way out. No way out. "Ahh, yeah..." he mumbled. "Friend from school."

Sara nodded at him, the movement itself a double entendre. "Yeah, she looked hot... You wouldn't want to share her would you? I could come over and we could party. You could watch." She smiled even wider, fluttering her eyelids. "Or whatever."

Thank god Billy Dornboss wasn't around or he'd demand Danny turn in his Man Card for not accepting the invitation. "Got an audition today?"

She stared at him. He pointed at the bag over her shoulder. "Oh this... yeah, rock video." She spun it around for him. It was a cheerleader outfit. For a child. A small child. "It's a high school theme thing. You know, tits and ass." (*He hated himself for picturing her in it.*) She smiled, then stood up straighter. "They never take me seriously. I'm a serious actress. I've got real credits. I was in the *Baywatch* movie."

Danny nodded vigorously. Almost painfully. "Yep, I know. Totally sucks. Hey, I gotta get to work, but good luck with your audition." He shoved past her, head down. Then spun on his heel, almost tripped backwards over the trash can.

She turned to watch him leave, one leg up, foot against the wall, knee and thigh presented, and she gave him what he could only interpret as her idea of a "sexy wave."

He started out the door. Sara gave Danny a sexy wave. "Let me know if you change your mind," she called.

Danny heard Billy's voice in his head, "*Burn that Man Card, loser.*"

THE WORKDAY WAS ENDLESS. A new collection came in but the new guys sorted every single album into the wrong category. Then some high school kids came in for the new Evans Swift and another of the new guys decided to put the new track on the store speaker. Then the regulars threatened to burn the place down. All the while, Danny checked his watch, witnessing time inch agonizingly closer to closing time.

With no small amount of shame, Danny worried about Laura like she was a new puppy. He was concerned what she'd chew on while he was gone. Or get into.

Finally, it was punch-out time. The TV in the little manager's office was tuned to the game. (That's how Danny thought of sports, when he thought of them at all. "What's on? 'The game'.") Same channel he'd left on for Laura. Halftime. The band was loud and the cheerleaders were hurling each other into orbit. Maybe watching that would be something Laura would like.

He honestly didn't know. He didn't know *anything* about her. She was still the ten year old girl he thought he'd killed, transformed into a beautiful, untouched creature watching 'the game' on his couch.

Dodging traffic, Danny hurried over to the little deli across the street, wondering if the fairy princess would prefer ham on rye or a turkey club.

Though it wasn't quite rush-hour, the deli was still packed. There was a long line of middle-aged men in ball caps checking their phones. Door-Dashers waited for food to deliver to someone else. The gig economy in action.

Full of nervous energy, Danny fidgeted in line, tried to distract himself with whatever was playing on the TV above the cash register. Some news thing, local-color. Well, Louisiana, apparently, so not that local.

Foot tapping, hands shoved into pockets, Danny forced himself to watch good ol' boy Remy

Boudreaux, three hundred pounds if he was an ounce, proud of his remaining three teeth, standing on his old Bayou shack, shotgun beside him, propped up idly against the door jamb. Danny couldn't be sure if this was real or some sort of satirical "news" show. Reality meant very little these days.

"—this he-yah is Da Republic of Boudrovia... as far as da eye can see... now is mine. I have made dis declaration... and I will enforce it."

Oh, goody, thought Danny. *Sovereign citizen right here.*

"It seems that the US Government might have something to say about that," the newscaster said, taking a swing at injecting reason into the moment and wondering how his journalistic career got him to this spot on the planet. "Aren't you worried that they'll just come in and arrest you?"

"Oh No," said Boudreaux, "my divine right to dis land comes from a very high power."

"You mean God?"

"Aw, Hell no... we'll leave him out of dis... I mean Big Bob... Here, I'll show ya... jus' follow me."

Clearly fearing for his safety, the newsman (and his presumably iron-spined cameraman) followed Boudreaux to the side of the shack. Danny waited in anticipation of the inevitable reveal of an enormous alligator or some such swamp critter.

Instead, Boudreaux waddled over to a tarp and swept it aside, dust and muck going everywhere, uncovering a large, rusty, cylindrical object. Across one side, paint peeling from the decades, was scrawled "BIG BOB."

The newscaster jumped back. "Oh my god.... that's an A Bomb!!!!

"Yep, I found it while I was gator hunting many

year back. See, dem fly boys dropped it accidental-like in the 1950s... Didn't go off... don't mean it won't... They looked high and low fo' it... Damned if it weren't right here all da time... well, welcome to Boudrovia..."

There was an abrupt cut to the newsroom. Two very pretty people sat stunned behind their rictus grins.

The girl behind the deli counter signaled to Danny that his order was up. He stepped forward, fumbling with his wallet. He didn't immediately hear the anchorperson choke out her throw to the next story. *"...Well, there's a story we'll keep an eye on. In other news, the police are asking for the public's help. A young woman named Laura Baxter who has disappeared from a local hospital..."*

Laura's name rang out and Danny dropped everything in his hands. Change went everywhere, the noise only drawing more attention to him. Like in a dream, Danny could hear the newscast, the sound wrapping around his head and beckoning to every one around him.

"Ms. Baxter suffers from a sleep disorder called parasomnia which renders her helpless most of the time. Authorities are afraid that she may have been kidnapped."

And then the TV image changed. No longer the static shot of the grinning mannequins at the desk. Now it was black and white shot, *just blurry enough,* of Danny. Pushing a wheel chair.

Wheeling Laura out of the hospital.

The newscaster's voice took on an ominous, echoey tone: *"As you can see from the security pictures it's difficult to see the man's face in the image. They believe the man to be an art student who had come to see Ms. Baxter on several occasions. The public is asked to help. If anyone has any information, they are encouraged to call the following number..."*

Abandoning his change, Danny gathered up his various bags and rushed out the door. The little bell above rang out and it sounded, to Danny, exactly like a police siren.

IT WAS uncanny and statistically impossible, but as soon as he stepped out of the elevator, he almost ran full tilt into Sara *again*. But she wasn't in a flirty mood. Her hair was pulled back in a vicious bun and her face likewise into a look of rage. Before he could ask, she shouted an explanation.

"Some motherfucking cocksucker broke into my place! I think they took a bunch of shit. I don't even know what!" She shoved past him into the elevator.

"Did you call the cops?"

"Duh, on the immediate. I'm going to get a better lock. Christ knows the super won't do shit about it."

As the doors slid shut, Danny heard his voice say, "Sorry to hear about..." but he had other things on his mind. Namely being the object of a manhunt.

Seeing that the door of his apartment was open, all the alarm bells of his body went off. Adrenaline and cortisol flooded his system. What predators had invaded? Cops? Doctors? Lawyers? Gorillas? Conflicting signals to his legs had him moving in a halting run which ended in a skid as he cautiously toed the door open.

Inside, all seemed quiet. Relatively. The TV was on at almost full blast, some infomercial selling a magical skin cream. No Laura.

Cereal box tipped over but not quite spilled. Empty box of Pop Tarts nearby. But no Laura.

Once upon a time he had a bat right inside the

door. Denise had taken it with her. Unarmed, Danny took a few more steps into the room.

His heart almost exploded when a blonde cheerleader burst out of his bedroom, pom poms fluffing furiously. Jumping up and landing in a "Ready" position, Laura screamed, "Gimme an A!"

Danny froze in place. His mouth opened. He heard himself say, "…A?"

It was the right answer. Laura beamed and jumped again, pom poms shedding whatever pom pom material comprised it. "Gimme a C!" It was the same red uniform Sara had brought in with her. Apparently, underwear had not been included in the costume, as Laura's jumps proved. *But how the hell did she get it?*

"Give me a Z! Give me an R! Gimme ah… ah, P! What's that spell?"

She beamed at him and waited. He did not say, "It doesn't spell anything." But it didn't matter. She leapt into his arms and answered her own question.

"Home," she said, nuzzling his neck. "Spells 'home'." Then she wrapped her arms around him and held him tight, like he was the comfort she'd always sought. *Him*, Danny Sloan. He held her back just as tightly.

Turning her face up to him, she seemed peaceful and safe. Tears came to his eyes in response. The moment was perfect. Then her smile turned sleepy and her eyes rolled back and she slid almost completely out of his arms. Danny fought momentum and gravity and ninety pounds of cheerleader to keep her off the floor.

And then there was a knock at the door. And Danny's heart attack returned. He screamed—too loud, too aggressive, too panicked—"*Be right there!*" Laura's limp body fought against his grasp, forced him to grab her arms and drag her into the bedroom.

The *knocking* turned into *pounding*.

"Hold on, I'm in the bathroom!" Danny screamed at the door. "Jesus fucking—*I'll be right there!*" Finally, he got the Laura's dead weight settled onto his bed.

The visitor either didn't hear him or intentionally ignored him, as the pounding became a bass drum beat. Danny could feel the thumping in his brain. "All right!" He closed the bedroom door behind him.

It's the cops. It has to be the cops. You got made, Danny. They know your face!

Hurrying to the door, he snagged the cereal box from the floor, managing to spill just a little more of the stale bits in the process. Because, of course he would. With a final leap, Danny slid the door open just a crack, ready for the battalion of cops to rain down upon him.

Instead, the barely-focused eyes of Billy Dornboss peered back at him through the gap. "Took you long enough," Billy said, his voice always a little higher when he was, well, high. "What's going on, dude? Are you holed up in here or something? You don't have enough money to be a recluse, Danny."

"No... just... on the john."

But Billy wasn't interested in the explanation. He pushed past Danny and walked an impressive straight line to the refrigerator. "Is this all you got?" In his hand, a singular Fresca, flavor unknown, leftover from a past party. "That's not... I didn't buy..." *Was that a noise from the bedroom?* The thought interrupted his babble. "Denise's," he concluded. "The store ran out of Cokes."

"And beer?"

"You're not allowed to drink on your meds."

The pop-and-hiss of the soda punctuated Billy's response: "I'm not *allowed* to do fucking anything. I just *do*." He took a big swallow from the can, his cheeks ballooned as he looked pointedly around the room. A big gulp, then a belch, as he toed the debris field left behind by Laura's food fest. "Danny maybe you do need a girlfriend. This place could stand a little tidying."

Did the bedroom door creak? "Huh? Yeah, so, so… How are you doing?"

"So, so…?" Billy mocked, then shrugged. "So-so." He took another swallow and then grimaced. "Working on finding a new place. Thought I'd go in with another artist and get something bigger, one of those lofts downtown."

With another glance at the door, Danny sat down in the hope it would prompt Billy to do the same. He didn't, preferring to lean against Danny's lone bookcase left behind by Hurricane Denise. "Yeah," Danny said. "That would be cool. I, uh… Yeah, I always dreamed of having a place like that."

The goddamned pom-pom is right there under the table! Right by Billy's goddamned foot!

Billy emptied the can then began to twang the tab. "You seen Sleeping Beauty lately?"

Danny's breath caught. "What? No… why?"

"You obviously haven't seen the news? Somebody kidnapped that chick."

"Kidnapped? Is that… that's how they're reporting it?

Billy stared for him for what seemed like a decade. He nodded and spoke slowly. "Yeah… Kid. Nap. *Ping*."

"Do they know who did it?"

Still flying on whatever he was on, Billy shrugged and rolled the back of his head along the wall like James Dean, staring at the ceiling but facing Danny's bedroom door. "Some sex pervert, no doubt. Some sad, demented, lonely loser who can only get it on with a chick when she's sleeping. Next step is serial killer."

Danny nearly tripped over—well, *everything*—in his haste to draw Billy's addled attention from the bedroom door. All he needed was for Laura to wake up, burst out, and lead the team to victory right in front of Billy. The movement at least registered on Billy's brain, and he shrugged before continuing his thought. "They have surveillance pictures but I guess their cameras are strictly Devonian Era shit... fuzzy. Could be anybody... could be me... could be you."

At that Danny laughed. It was a coughing bray that was too loud to have been genuinely motivated by humor. "Right, sure. Can you imagine me kidnapping anybody? Or... you? Right? You'd pass out on top of her."

Billy stared at him, eyes semi-focused. "Rude," he said. "But, yeah, that would be fucked up." He yawned wide, stretched, let his head roll on his neck, and again he wound up facing the bedroom door. And Danny was *certain* he saw a shadow pass the gap. "Hey, uh," he said, throwing an arm across Billy's shoulders. It was the friendliest way he could think of to steer him away. "Uh, I'm sorry to break this up. See, I've got some research I've got to get done. So I, ah, kinda need to get to work."

Danny opened the door. Billy slapped his hand against the jamb and stopped moving. "What *research*?"

"Records," Danny said, after an interminable pause. "There's some records I need to find for a customer..."

Nodding, Billy held up a finger, then turned it

into a finger-gun. "No problem. I myself enjoy nocturnal activities." Billy's door-stop face split into a wide smile. The finger gun transformed, this time into a waggle of judgment. "Danny... I know what's going on here."

"What... what, uh, do you mean?"

Billy pointed his chin towards the middle distance and asked, in a sing-song voice, "Who's the cheerleader?"

Danny turned in the vague direction: *I knew it! The god... damned... pom-pom!* He forced a smile. One with too many teeth and implied immorality. "Oh! Oh yeah. I met her at school."

Billy's smile matched, then exceeded, the lasciviousness he inferred. "Art school cheerleader. Rooting for the live models. Keeping up morale in ceramics." He slapped Danny in the chest. "I bet she did her whole routine for you. Watch out, bud. Hey, win one for the Gipper, will ya?" Another affectionate tap to Danny's sternum, this time with knuckles, and with his face gone somber. "Just remember, Danny Boy, while the pipes, the pipes are callin'... Women treat men just like Gods... They worship us... Dance for us... Sing to us... Exalt us... then they're always pestering us to do shit for them..."

Danny let him continue his rant from the other side of the door.

CHAPTER 13

There's a crooked house up on that sharp steep hill. Lightning crashes around it always. It wants to crumble to dust, but the Ash World won't let it die. This is where *it* lives. The scarier *it*—scarier than the worm that crawled into Laura's brain and called itself Volpe.

She runs and she runs and she runs but the mirrors turn and hide the path before her. The mirrors capture her hundreds of times over, keep aspects of her trapped inside the metallic glass. Hundred and hundreds of Lauras weeping and screaming for freedom. One image freezes as the mirror spins and out steps the worm, Volpe, in his Demon Form, his eyes of black fire and his cracking skin and burning bones within. His arm whip out; pindly glistening fingers fly at her, grabbing her skull. He forces her head to turn, almost fully around, to stare at the hateful house.

"That is where your fear dwells…" comes that oily, slithery voice licking the inside ot her mind. "That is the home of the Clouded Man."

The Clouded Man. The Clouded Man.

The Clouded Man has branches for hair, growing out of his scalp like the roots of a potato.

Its eyes and mouth are black hollow tunnels, but something gleams back from the empty sockets. Not eyes. Something *other* than eyes. And its skin is white, mottled, soft, yielding, like the writhing flesh of a maggot. Yet somehow its touch draws blood.

Laura cries out in anguish as the Clouded Man's talons sink into her head, drawing blood from where his fingers have dug in. She can feel the fingers piercing her skull, then her brain, then her mind, forcing her eyes to roll up and see the damage being done.

Volpe's ugly horrible voice slides and slithers over her mind, probing and caressing in ways she'd never, ever wants to be touched. "I will love you..." it whispers, and like a cat's tongue, the voice is rough and wet. "I will save you from him. I will save you from The Clouded Man. If you want me to." The voice seems to dance over her brain, slide a finger down the cleft between hemispheres. "But there are things you must do for me."

Blood fills her mouth. She has to open her lips to keep from drowning.

In the mirror, Volpe caresses her body, as his voice caresses her mind. He tells her everything he would do to her should she not obey. He would do things to her that no child should suffer. He shows her things that make her ill, even worse than watching what his hands do to her body as his whisper assaults her senses. She cries. The tears are blood. All is blood.

The mirror spins again, making its hideous sound of metal piercing glass. Gone are Laura and Volpe. In their place is Danny. He bangs his hands against the inside of the mirror and begs her to *wake up—*

The burst of terror popped Danny's eyes open. *Where the fuck am I?* He'd been dreaming of Laura and a blackened land of spinning mirrors. Of a giant maggot with a human face…

Disoriented, he was only dimly aware that a weight was pressing down on him. His skin registered the familiar scratch of the ugly couch. He'd fallen asleep—like actual, *for real sleep*, nightmares be damned—but what was on top of him? What was holding him down? What was—?

Finally, he wriggled onto his back, looked up to see Laura sitting on top of him, smiling somebody else's smile, her bright white teeth gleaming through a mask of blood.

So much blood. The cheerleader outfit was glued to her skin.

In her right hand was a butcher knife. Danny didn't own a butcher knife.

She lunged at him—fright took his breath away. So close, their noses touched. Her smile was so wide and the stench of blood was even on her breath as she whispered into his gaping mouth: "Tick, Tick, Tick!"

With the words came more blood, spilling from her mouth, dribbling over her chin and into his face. Before he could even cry out, Danny saw the knife coming towards his face. He managed to swing his head away just before the blade stabbed into the couch arm. "Tick! Tick! Tick!" she cried, stabbing down again. And again.

In both fight and flight, Danny thrashed beneath her, dodging the knife—Left! Right! "Laura, wake up!"

Instead, she reared up with the knife grasped in both hands—it gave him enough leverage to squirm out from under her. He landed hard on the floor and crab-walked away from the crazed woman.

Laura didn't pursue him. Her eyes were open but she was clearly still asleep as she stabbed into the couch, over and over, in sheer horrible violence. Puffs of stuffing and pillow feathers swirled around her, like a horrible snow. Not looking at him. Not looking *for* him. Just intent on murdering *something* in her dream.

He let a few moments pass before taking a few cautious steps towards her. If she registered his movement, she didn't let on beyond slowing the stabbing. The violence decreased as her strength waned. Or perhaps it was her interest. Her right hand fell away from the knife handle, hung limp at her side while the left rose, then hesitated. Danny took the opportunity to gently pry the knife from her hand. By now the blade was blunt, the tip curled. It had been a cheap knife, but that wouldn't have been a comfort had it found his jugular. He tossed it away and it clattered into the kitchen area.

Sitting down beside her, Danny waved his hand before her unseeing eyes. No reaction.

"Still asleep," he muttered. With a sigh, he started to gather her into his arms. "Okay, let's get you back into—"

Laura's head swiveled around and her eyes were wide. And dark. Without any white showing. Different, too, was the voice that hissed from her open mouth, not articulating, just a sourceless echo clawing its way out of her throat: "In time she's mine... She's mine in time..."

Then she howled and lunged at him again. They fell to the floor and she wound up straddling him, her hands fixed into claws, eyes open wide but not seeing.

A snarl escaped her lips.

"Laura!"

The blackness vanished from her eyes, now properly blue and white with awareness. Then her face contorted into horror as she saw all the blood, all over her, everywhere.

What came from her throat might have become a scream had sleep not taken her first.

CHAPTER 14

WHAT DID YOU DO, LAURA? JESUS GOD, WHAT DID you do?

There was so much blood, Danny didn't know where to start cleaning. There wasn't a clean place on the floor to lay Laura down—the bathtub was *still* filled with records. What parts of his brain weren't on fire with panic were simply exhausted lumps of gray matter. Nothing was functioning properly.

The cheerleader uniform was soggy with blood and it *squelched* as he stripped it from her body. Blood had soaked through and stained her all over, leaving her looking like a Dalmatian with port-wine birthmarks. *Whatever*, his brain wasn't working. Laura's body, nude, beautiful, just another surface to clean.

He sponged her down, then mopped around her, got her dried off and into one of his old dress shirts, which fit her like a small tent. Finally, he got her into bed. Only then did he start to cry.

She woke up at the end, just as he tightened the final knot around the post at the foot of the bed. He gave it a test yank and saw her foot twitch.

Laura's eyes were wide open then, filled with

confusion and fear, but not terror. There was still trust in the deep blue eyes. "Hospital?" she asked.

Guilt wouldn't let him respond at first. Just a nod. Finally, "No, no hospital. Home. Still."

She looked to the clothesline knots keeping her from moving her arms and legs. He'd wrapped the wrists and ankles with cloth so that the rope wouldn't chafe her skin.

Her fingertips were still stained a faint red. "Did I do wrong?"

Guilt again. And deep sorrow. "No," Danny said. "I did."

Feeling suddenly very heavy, Danny sat down on the edge of the bed. He needed to explain to her his thinking. That this was for the best. She tried to *sleep-stab* him, after all. How do you tell someone who spent her entire life asleep that she wasn't *in* danger, but that she *was* the danger? That she could—

Outside his door, someone screamed.

Danny swore that he felt his heart stop.

Another scream, then the sound of panicked, running footsteps. Unusual for his building. Ever.

Impossibly, his mouth went even drier, his tongue plastered to his hard palate. Looking down, he saw Laura's wide eyes, her concern matching his. He put a finger to his lips and slowly got up from the bed. Insanely, he didn't want his movement to attract any outside attention.

"Please, don't leave me," Laura whispered, but he didn't hear.

He cracked the door and let in another scream from without: "Oh, sweet Jesus! Help! Somebody call the police!"

It was his neighbor, Mrs.... Something. Something Polish maybe? Her face was both sheet-white and, somehow, beet red, as she swooned in the hallway. "Call 9-11! Call 9-11!" she screamed as she staggered towards the elevators.

Slowly, Danny emerged from his apartment, like a groundhog scared of seeing his shadow. Already, other neighbors whose names he didn't know—he'd only lived there for eight years, after all—went running past, all heading for one apartment.

Sara's apartment.

As they took turns peering through Sara's open door, the other neighbors screamed too, another little old lady crossed herself, and the old man next to her spat on the floor to ward off evil. Too little, too late, Danny surmised. The gathering was like a beating heart, crowding around the open door, then stepping away just as quickly, dancing between curiosity and revulsion.

Danny took his time. Partly, he didn't want to attract attention. Primarily, he didn't want to see inside Sara's room. He didn't want to know how Laura obtained Sara's costume.

Light coming through the door was constantly changing—bright, dark, dim, brighter. The Little Old Floor Spitter tried to stop him, but Danny pushed past him and looked inside.

All of Sara's haute catalog furniture had been shoved against the walls, making a clearing in the middle of her living room. In the open space was a straight back wooden chair. In the chair was Sara, facing the door to greet the neighbors.

Naked.

Lashed to the chair with belts, her final accessories, some rhinestone sparkling between the glops of blood.

Eyes open, staring, empty. Her mouth smiled wide. It had been carved that way.

The muted TV was the source of the fluctuating light, scanning channels one after another, never staying for more than a second. Because the remote was in Sara's hand. Held there with a wrap of duct tape.

Sara's head was taped up to the back of the chair, to keep her attention fixed to a message scrawled in her own blood above her doorway:

TICK TICK TICK

The next few seconds were longer than hours and didn't seem to be happening in order.

People screamed.

Danny turned back towards his apartment.

Laura did this.

TICK TICK TICK

There were police sirens in the distance. The far distance. The middle distance. The Doppler effect in action.

It's a dream. It's a bad, bad dream…

Was the hallway always this long?

Sara, nude, tortured, dead.

He could hear more people running behind him, shouting, crying, all heading to see the Amazing Murdered Sara.

Sara *Something.*

He'd only known her for three years.

Sara *Baker? Sumner? Beckett? Montgomery?*

Sara Dead.

Sara Dead. Dead. Dead.

Two other anonymous neighbors shouldered him just as he reached his door, but the jostles didn't register. Slipping Inside, he closed his door behind him, sealing it off from the outside world. From the hallway that lead to Sara Dead Dead Dead.

Inside, Laura was asleep in his hallway. He couldn't be sure, but she might have *chewed* through the rope at her right wrist. He couldn't

blame her. He'd dragged her into this nightmare.
The same one he'd dragged himself into.

Outside his window red and blue lights flashed
their alert.

Not Christmas. Not the Fourth of July.

Murder.

Come and celebrate the murder.

Was he high enough up that a fall from the
window would kill him?

Red. Blue. Red. Blue. Red—

His cell phone rang louder than it ever had, jolting
him from the pocket of his sweatshirt like an exposed
wire. Swearing, he fumbled for the demanding object.
Saw the caller: BILLY DORNBOSS. His bestest stalker.

His brain was still relaying the information as
he answered, "Yeah…?"

The tinny voice was filled with irritation. "Hey,
what the hell's going on over there?"

Danny's brain finally updated. "Billy," he said
dully.

"*Yeah*, it's Billy. Are you screening your calls or
what? Busy with your cheerleader?"

Danny barely heard. "Yeah."

"Well… anyway, I bumped into one of your
vinyl junkies… a guy named Phil."

*Phil… Phil… who the fuck was Phil? Who gives a
shit about Phil right now? Sara is dead!*

"Yeah."

"He gave me a record to give you," said Billy's
voice, coming from far away. Maybe from the past.
"I just thought I'd come by and drop it off, but
wanted to call and make sure weren't in the middle
of any pom pom action."

"Yeah," said Danny, mouth and brain almost in
synch. "Now isn't a really good time, Bill. Let's
hook up later… yeah?"

"You sound weird," Distant Past Billy responded. "What's going on over there? I'm coming over."

No! Fuck off! "Billy, don't come over."

"Why? You in some kind of trouble?"

You were just fucking here! Go get a fix and leave me alone! "No, there's been... a break-in at one of the other apartments. I think the police are going to show up."

Clearly it was a night of comedy for the Divine, because right on cue, there was a loud knock at his door.

"See? That's them. Gotta go."

Distant Billy shouted, "Wait!" and then was silenced.

Danny's eyes shot from the door to the hallway with the sleeping girl who'd clearly been restrained, probably against her will. You know, the *famous one.*

More knocking, becoming pounding, accompanied by an aggravated voice. "Yo, police, anyone home?"

Rushing over to Laura, he dropped his phone and it immediately bounced to someplace inaccessible. "Just a minute... I'm on the phone—be right there!" Again, he struggled with the sleeping princess to drag her back to bed. You know, like in all the best fairy tales.

DETECTIVE GARRETT COCKED an eyebrow at Detective Conroy. "He's on the phone."

Conroy shrugged. "Who isn't these days?"

They were both in the middle of nicotine fidgets, exacerbated by the caffeine shakes, so they were feeling their best to look at yet another sliced up young girl.

Conroy gave the uniformed officer a vague nod, telling him without telling him to wait for the guy on the phone to come out of his apartment. He couldn't be sure, but Conroy suspected, given the look the uniform returned, he was "telling him without telling him" to "go fuck himself." And he could respect that. The rumpled pair of detectives started down the hall. Anyone would wonder how long they'd been married.

"Aren't you supposed to be on vacation, Hank?" asked Garrett.

"I'm *on* my vacation," said Conroy. "I'm having a great time."

Behind them, they heard the door creak open, and a jittery voice ask, "What is it? Did something happen?" but neither could be bothered to turn around. The uniform would take the statement.

"Fuck," said Garrett, "this is not a way to start the day..." Forensics in their white uniforms were gathering in the corners of the dim apartment. They looked like ghostly Oompa Loompas. "Has anybody touched anything?"

"No, sir," another uniformed officer responded.

Garrett nodded. That was *something* at least. He took in the scene. His stomach was already sour, his ulcer, a longtime friend, expelled some acid to express its opinion on matters.

Looking up at the lintel, Garrett read the words out loud, "Tick Tick Tick." He repeated it, almost absent-mindedly.

"What's that mean?" asked the uniform.

"That his watch is working." Garrett bent down close to examine the wounds that comprised Sara's face. He sighed, long and hard, to fully express the depth of his exhaustion. Down to the soul. "It means it's going to be a long day," he said, standing and stretching. "I swear to God... Why is it always Monday? Why can't they wait and spread it out over the week?"

"Because you're suppose to suffer," said Conroy, finally gracing the crime scene with his presence. "'Cause this is purgatory for some past crime in another life." Conroy took a deep breath and let it out in one long continuous sigh, one-upping Garrett's. "I'm guessing this is not a 'the boyfriend did it' situation."

"Hank, no. No, I know what you're thinking," said Garrett. "It can't be him. He's still locked up. I just talked to the hospital a couple of minutes ago."

Conroy rolled his eyes and it looked painful. "Being locked up means nothing to this guy. For all we know he talked somebody into doing this."

"Who? Squeaky Fromme?"

Conroy shook his head, jowly, like a bulldog. "Look, I hope that you're right. This guy, he only cares about two things: his book store and himself... And that book store went under."

Garrett didn't respond right away. When he did, it almost sounded out of context. "Three things."

Conroy turned from examining a blood splatter while an Oompa Loompa tried to dance around him. "What?"

"Volpe," said Garrett. "He cares about *three things*. You're forgetting about the girl."

"What girl?"

"Laura Baxter."

"Oh, yeah," Conroy nodded, "the sleepy girl."

"Yeah. He cares about her."

"Okay, three things."

The pair left the apartment, almost in unison. They looked at the hallway full of confused tenants and open doors.

"Which rooms do you want," asked Garrett. "Odd numbers or even?"

"Odd," said Conroy.

"How'd I know?"

ALL THE UNIFORMED officer did was take down Danny's name and cell number then left him alone. Danny took the opportunity to further clean the apartment so it looked less like its own crime scene. He kept his thoughts focused on the task at hand—cleaning, mopping, wiping, polishing—so that he didn't have to think about Laura.

Laura standing over Sara, carving her face into a smile.

He'd gotten her back into bed and didn't bother with the ropes. Last time, they didn't even slow her down.

Renewed pounding on his door turned his blood into wet cement. "Yeah!" he shouted back. Closing the bedroom door, he prayed to whoever to just *let her sleep.*

"Detective Conroy, police," said the big bulldog in the hallway. "Daniel Sloan?"

Danny tried to will composure as he opened the door. "Yes?" he asked, as innocently as he could.

"Detective Conroy," the bulldog said again. "Can I come in? I need to ask you a few questions."

Danny peered past the big cop into the hallway. Most of the neighbors had returned to their rooms and the space was relatively free of police. Just another plainclothes guy at the other end of the hall talking to Mrs. Something Polish who'd found Lisa's body.

"What about?" Danny asked, faking ignorance. (Possibly.)

Conroy's voice was flat. "It'll only take a minute," he said as he pushed his way inside.

The big cop, in his big cliché of a trench coat, his little cliché of a flip notebook, was used to dominating every space he was in. Without looking at Danny, he immediately surveyed the room.

Danny couldn't be sure, but he *might* have heard the bedroom door's familiar *creak-crack* of the hinges.

Both men were thinking: *Something's wrong. Something's wrong.*

"What's back there?" asked Conroy.

Just a young woman I kidnapped and tied to a bed because she sliced up my neighbor and then tried to carve me up too. "Just the bedroom," said Danny. "My bedroom."

"You live by yourself?"

Danny nodded, then realized the Detective couldn't actually hear a nod. "Usually," he said.

Usually? What the hell are you doing? Get him away from the door!

Conroy continued to take in the scenery. Danny couldn't tell what had attracted the big man's attention. Was 'cop intuition' a real thing? Wasn't that just on TV? He strained to see around the cop. The bedroom door was *wide open*.

And empty.

Clearly, definitively empty.

Finally, the man shrugged and turned his back to the dim hallway.

He made a sound. It could have been a belch or a swallowed sneeze. "That's odd…"

But he was looking at nothing. His eyes were wide open, but they took in nothing.

Just like Sara.

There was a trickle of blood from his nostril, then it quickly became a running stream. The big cop wobbled unsteadily on his feet—then lurched backwards in sudden violence. Conroy's face contorted into a mask of blind pain, arms flailing behind him, trying to dislodge something he couldn't reach, like a very bad itch. Just as suddenly, he dropped hard to his knees, blood pumped from the deep wound in the center of his back.

There was Laura, behind him the whole time, crouched in the dark and waiting to spring. Just as the Voice in her head commanded her to. She held the knife up for Danny to see. Her eyes were wide, but they weren't looking at him. She was far, far away.

The voice that came from her mouth wasn't her own.

"Tick, Tick, Tick, tick, tick, ti—"

Like a striking cobra, Laura lunged at the kneeling cop and stabbed him again, deep and just above his groin. Then, like gutting a turkey, she slid the blade up. Until it hit bone.

Danny's body recoiled in terrified sympathy. His brain rejected the image before him: Laura showered in gore, Conroy's insides spilling out (*I just cleaned there!*) across his floor, while he tried, with a stupid expression, to hold himself together. Conroy's mouth opened and closed, but only a gurgling moan came out. When he finally collapsed to the floor, it was as if someone had dropped a garbage bag of tomato soup. Conroy splattered everywhere.

While Danny watched, Laura's bloody face transformed from psychotic glee to frightened bewilderment. Looking up at him, not comprehending, Laura let the knife drop from her hands. It clattered onto the floor, splashing more Conroy about.

With begging eyes, hands reaching for him, she said, "…Danny?"

Then sleep took her again.

Something in Danny's brain broke then. Later, he'd be unable to recall the hours immediately after Conroy's murder.

Just the shameful knowledge that he fled his apartment, leaving Laura asleep on the floor, in a puddle of dead cop.

CHAPTER 15

Laura's eyes fluttered open and her mind rejected the world. *Blood? Why? Danny?*

Her thoughts wouldn't come out as words. She crab-walked away from the dead man on the floor, away from the knife in the center of the expanding puddle of red blood.

The smell was awful. Like... like... *shit*. Blood and *shit* and she wasn't supposed to say that word, she didn't think. But that was it. That was the smell. Shit and just nasty... Nasty...

She found her voice and its urgency: "Danny?"

Where did this dress come from? Where was the pretty red uniform? Where was Danny?

The dress, her hands, her legs—all smeared with blood. With the dead man's blood. It was all over everywhere.

Scrambling to her feet, she tried to wipe the blood away, but there wasn't a clean spot on the dress. Unable to catch her breath, she panted and choked and wiped her hands on the chair, on the drapes, on cleanish spots on Danny's only rug. Tears burned her eyes, ran hot down her cheeks. *Where was Danny? Where—?*

For most of what she thought of as "her life,"

Laura knew Hospital and Lauraland. Recently, the Horrible Ash Place had become her third world. Where was she now? If Danny wasn't here… was she…?

Was she… was she in *Danny's Dream?*

This is where Danny brought her: this room, this place. If the place was here and Danny wasn't… she *had* to be in his dream.

Okay… I just need to find where he's sleeping.

The thoughts made perfect sense to her. If she was in Danny's dream, he could lead her out again. She had to trust that he would dream her the right path to find him. She knew, then, that she shouldn't leave the room like this. The Other Dreams in Danny's Dream might get upset or scared and might try to hurt her. She didn't know if she *could* be hurt in Danny's dream.

But in Danny's dream, the floor was hard, and corners were sharp, and there was a dead man making a stink and she needed to leave the room. There was a big coat hanging on the closet doorknob. It was scratchy on her bare skin, but it hid the blood. The sneakers by the door were too big for her feet, but made the walking softer, even though they flapped like duck feet. It was better than nothing, she decided.

Taking a deep breath, Laura took her first steps outside the room.

The hallway was familiar. She *had* been in Danny's dream. That's where the nice lady had that pretty costume and didn't say anything when she asked to borrow it. The nice lady hadn't said anything to Laura at all. Not even when the knife—

Fear shot through Laura, making her stomach knot up, and her back feel cold. She didn't want to think of the lady, or the knife, or the dead man— why was Danny's dream so scary?

Voices.

They were coming down the hallway, coming towards her. Getting louder. Scary voices. Men angry, rushing. Their footsteps were heavy and echoey in the hall. They were coming around the corner.

Breath hitching, Laura turned around and ran from the voices. She didn't know the word "Stairs", but she recognized the zigzag symbol and the stick figure walking "down." The voices weren't as loud here, which meant the men weren't behind that door.

Down. Down. Down. Her shoes flapped along the steps and made funny squeaking noises beneath her bare feet. But she was scared and didn't want to laugh. It was dark and where there was light, the bulbs flickered and made the light scarier. Finally, at the bottom: there was another door.

The door was heavy and she had to push hard, but then:

Outside.

Danny's dream had an outside. It was *loud*.

Danny's dream had a *morning*.

Lauraland was always sunny. The light almost never changed, even when it rained its dry rain that was cold against her skin but never *wet*.

Danny's dream had chilly air that raised goofbumps on her skin.

She was outside, between two buildings, and the ground was messy with trash and stuff, and everything was so *loud*. Cars beeping and machinery yelling and people yelling and more people yelling.

She had to find Danny.

She didn't know who Detective Garrett was when she passed him on the sidewalk.

DETECTIVE GARRETT DIDN'T RECOGNIZE *her* either. And he'd kick himself later.

For, in the ten minutes it took for Det. Jeff Garrett to wrap his last door-knock interview (*'Din't hear nuthin'.*), take the rattling elevator to the lobby, cross the street, grab a pack of Marlboros from the bodega, and cross back, an unknown assailant managed to gut Detective Hank Conroy from throat to groin, spill him across the apartment, and flee, presumably gore-soaked, without anyone seeing or hearing a thing.

The last part didn't surprise him. His grief did.

They'd both been on the squad for roughly the same amount of time over two decades. Garrett had made his grade in New York City; Conroy in Los Angeles. They'd seen their share of weird shit and more or less bonded over that, in as much as they were capable, anyway.

Over the last twenty, they'd partnered up for this heinous thing or that. Long stakeouts over stale coffee, trapped in each other's air. They shared 'weird shit' stories to pass the time.

"There was a haunted website," said Garrett on one of these long-ass bull sessions. "Run by a serial killer's ghost."

"Sure," said Conroy, unimpressed.

"I was a uniform in Queens," Garrett went on. "Watched this detective first-grade go completely nuts over the idea that a serial killer's skull film brought the victim's ghost back to life on the internet."

"Why not?"

"Guess the killer?"

"Nephew of the Son of Sam."

"Alistair Pratt."

"FBI Most Wanted and Prom Queen of 2001 Alistair Pratt?"

"2002," said Garrett.

"Did ya get him?"

"I was part of the cleanup crew. I got to see the bodies."

"How many?"

"Four, but it took a while to sort out the pieces."

Conroy belched, possibly in approval, but ready to one-up. "*Syngenor*," he said.

"Gehsundheit," said Garrett.

Conroy spelled it out and used his hands: "*Syn*-thesized *Gen*-etic *Or*-ganism. Syngenor."

"Suitable for a boy or a girl."

"Detective Lou Capell was convinced this was a kind of science experiment gone wrong, that it lived in the L.A. sewers, emerged at night in search of—you ready? Human spinal fluid."

"Couldn't it just go to Chinatown?"

"That's what *I* said." Conroy drained his coffee, tried and failed to get the oversized mug to sit comfortably in the cup-holder, as he always did. "I get called in to back up Lou at a metal shop. *He* claims he shot this lizard-looking motherfucker and knocks it into a drop forge."

"A what?"

"Like a metal forge. A big well."

Garrett lit his zillionth cigarette of the night. "Okay."

"And yeah, the bottom of that thing is just covered in blood and ooze and vile shit. The only other witness is a chick in a coma. When she wakes up, she's totally insane."

"We should write a book. *Campfire Tales for Cops.*"

"We'd sell dozens of copies."

Garrett had no idea if Conroy was still married. He couldn't remember if he'd ever mentioned having kids. Or even a pet. He may have mentioned still liking the Yankees.

Gallows humor, ghost stories, Pratt, Volpe, Syngenor... that's what had made them good partners.

Twenty-some years, undone in ten minutes.

By some goddamned motherfucking monster.

Without tearing his eyes away from the remains of his (friend?) sometimes partner, Garrett addressed the uniformed officer lingering by the door, waiting for instructions. "Who lives here?"

"An art student named Daniel Sloan," said the officer.

"Find him," Garrett said. The officer left quietly. The detective's jaw ached. He'd been clenching it again. Have to wear the mouthpiece tonight. Wake up drowning in drool.

His thoughts organized themselves as he scanned the room, looking everywhere else now, beyond Conroy's corpse. *Daniel Sloan. Art student. Collects records. Sparse furniture.*

...and a cheerleader's pom pom right there on the floor.

CHAPTER 16

Danny's dream was so loud, Laura had to cover her ears with her hands. A big vehicle blared and bellowed as it passed, it made her scream and take shelter in a doorway. She crouched down and waited for the big car-thing to pass.

People, too, passed her. Some looked at her, but no one said a word to her. No one offered her help or, it seemed, harm. Because, of course, they lived in Danny's dream. They were *his* Dream People. Maybe those two old people on the bench over there were *Danny's* mommy and daddy.

So, *of course*, they couldn't hurt her. She was just visiting.

"Okay," she said, out loud, to Danny's World. "Okay, I'll come find you!"

The morning light was getting brighter, and it seemed like Danny's World was waking up with it. Up ahead and around a corner, she could hear more of Danny's Dream People, and she wanted to see what Dannyland looked like.

No rotating mirrors, that was for sure. And no Clouded Man with sticks for hair and holes for eyes. Just... people. Like... *people* people. Like Hospital people. They felt real when she bumped them.

Sometimes they said, "Excuse me." The talking ones, Laura guessed. Not all of the people in Lauraland talk. Sometimes they looked like people from Hospital.

She looked at each face as she passed, but she didn't see Hospital faces. There were definitely Danny People. The Danny People were going in and out of buildings—*stores*! They were going to *stores*! She'd only *heard* of stores. Where people go and buy things like... food... and sneakers... *things*. Danny's Dream was so big!

There was a lady with white hair and a face made of wrinkles and she was walking a big ol' doggy that was all fur and smiles and a big wet nose. Laura could barely see his eyes under all that fluff. It made her laugh with joy.

"Hi! Look at you! Hi, Teddy Bear... You are sooo beautiful."

The lady was so much shorter than Laura and smiled up at her. "You can pet him if you want. His name is George."

"George?" One of the people in Hospital was named George! Laura reached out to the dog. "Hi, George!" And George let her bury her hands into his warm soft fur. "Thank you, George! Thank you... lady."

Danny's Dream People were *so nice*. But of course they would be. Danny was nice. And he was tall. And he was handsome. Like a prince. Like a *king.* He was King, because this was Dannyland.

She liked that word. Dannyland. She couldn't wait until he could see Lauraland. It wasn't as big, of course. But it was nice and Danny would like it.

Danny would...

Shit, even in Dannyland, I can still get sleepy.

Her sneakers felt big and heavy on her feet. Maybe if she just sat down, she wouldn't go anywhere. She could stay in Dannyland until she found Danny. *Then* they could sleep next to each other.

All the *stores* she passed had big windows that had ghostly Lauras in them. The Ghost Lauras moved like she did. The Ghost Lauras seemed sleepy too.

One Ghost Laura seemed to wave to her from a big window. Behind that big window were row after row of big fluffy beds. Ghost Laura smiled and Real Laura smiled back. It was just what she needed. Like magic!

Dannyland was so cool!

It was dark when Danny fled his apartment. When he stepped off the metro, morning light screamed at him in a stark reminder of reality. He didn't remember the ride. He didn't even remember getting on the train in the first place. But there he was: staring up at the massive and decrepit old warehouse Billy Dornboss called his "studio." In an area called "The Docks," though that kind of commerce didn't go on much any more.

The Docks were more or less the bohemian section of town. SoHo for the Not-So. Greenwich for the mean and lean. Billy's studio was a perfect example of Brutalism: a short, squat building that looked like it could withstand a nuclear blast—and *had,* considering there wasn't an unbroken window to be found. It had heat and light and nobody quite knew who owned it or how Billy afforded it.

But, then again, nobody knew much about Billy's family, or if any tales of his old man's "shady dealings" were real. Depending on his drug-of-the-moment, Billy could spin yarns of mobster uncles and career criminal grandmothers. Maybe the studio was just some Dornboss family write-off no longer needed for illicit means.

Or maybe the guy was just squatting there. You never could tell with Billy Dornboss.

Standing in the street and staring at the ugly-ass building, Danny wondered what part of his lizard brain thought that he would find any kind of comfort or safety at the studio, but like an addled homing pigeon, he found his way to the one person he truly thought of as a friend. A drunk, schizo, kleptomaniac, anarchist, petty criminal, but *friend* nonetheless.

A Volkswagen barked an angry bleat at him, ordering him to move from the street. It was enough to jog Danny's brain out of autopilot.

OVER THE YEARS, Billy had obsessed over developing his *style*, but it was only when he discovered his *medium* did his vision truly take shape. He wanted his art to give breath and form to his anxieties and fears, his loathing of society. He wanted his art to *piss right in the eyes of society*. In fact, that had been the theme of his first installation. (Although, really, it should have been titled "I Snorted Crystal and Haven't Slept in Six Days.")

Since his nightmares were *huge* and his anxieties were *legendary*, his art could be nothing short of *gigantic*. With sheet metal, clockwork gears, and tagger spray paint, he could bring his hate to motherfuckin' *life*.

When you walked into the studio, you were greeted with metal figures moving in precise mechanical precision, some waving and smiling with demented faces, many with eyes of spinning hypnotist pinwheels. Villains encouraging you to *con-*

sume, conform, revel in repetition. Billy the God had created his people in the image he *wanted them to have.*

His last installation, "The Art of the Automaton," had featured a trio of mecha-men in top hats, eyes spinning like hypno-wheels. They did a little dance and bowed in unison. The critics called it "a cute homage to the automatons of Thomas Kuntz," which should have been a compliment, but only reinforced his rage.

After leaving Danny's apartment, Billy returned to the studio intending to work on his latest, THE METAL MAN. The METAL MAN was eight feet tall by now, with Billy continuing to weld on new bits and filigree and flash, and it still wasn't perfect. He'd had to haul out the giant scaffolding ladder, the one with the bad locking wheel, just to reach the top of the METAL MAN's head. It needed a new spinning eyeball.

But during the bus ride home, Billy had an epiphany. He saw Volpe's face clearly in his mind, and then the entire scene unfolded before him. He saw it all: a mechanical show-stopper out of Victorian magic shows. Transmogrification, transformation, teleportation. He had the gears, the hydraulics, he even had a porcelain phrenology bust just dying to be incorporated into the madness.

By the time the bus reached his neighborhood, Billy was vibrating with inspiration. He wouldn't need anything tonight. Not crystal, not even coffee. He was high on his own creative dopamine—and wasn't *that* the dream?

Less than an hour in, a pair of cops in ugly suits swung by to interrupt him, asking all sorts of questions about Danny. Danny, Danny, Danny, they wanted to know. Who was he and what was he and when was the last time you saw him and when was the last time you witnessed him tear up a parking ticket, or whatever. Billy never talked to cops. It was a hard and fast rule.

Tonight he was busy and inspired and way too sober to even mess with cops. He stood at the door and stonewalled them. What were they gonna do? Lock him up? That doesn't *stop* Billy Dornboss. It just *delays* him.

Eventually they sleazed away, leaving their cards behind along with a series of veiled threats. All that Billy took away was a sense of dread that his buddy—his *only* buddy—had gotten himself into a world of shit. All he could do was occupy his flying mind. Worrying wouldn't do anyone any good.

He'd just begun applying flame to metal when the room came to life with the sound of female ecstasy—fast and sharp, almost yipping towards a sustained panting scream.

His doorbell. Recorded from a Jenna Jameson porno. Because why wouldn't Billy Dornboss have a doorbell like that?

He only ever got two visitors: Danny and Bozo, his dealer. He'd just bought some rock from Bozo yesterday, so it must be Danny at the door.

Danny was at the door, indeed. Looking more fucked up than Billy had ever seen him.

"Danny, Jesus, what the fuck are you doing here?" he grabbed the front of Danny's hoodie and yanked him through the big sliding door. "Half the planet is looking for you, man. The cops were here." He had no idea why he was suddenly taking this shit seriously. Seeing Danny in the flesh had set off some sort of alarm in Billy's nervous system, cutting through the haze.

"I told them I hadn't seen you since I got out of rehab, but I don't think they believed me. They think you're the next Zodiac or something. Did anybody see you when you came in here?"

"I…" Danny stood trancelike just inside the door. The doorbell had brought all the mechanicals to life. The movement and tinny noise overwhelmed him. "I don't know."

"You don't know," said Billy, peering around his door, searching the dark for coppers lurking in the shrubbery. "It's great that you don't know. The less information the better, that's my motto."

Billy slid the door shut. The click of the lock echoed through the space, adding to the metallic cacophony. There was a big dramatic red kill switch on the wall and Billy punched it with his fist. All the mechanicals went back to sleep.

With a thousand-yard stare, Danny surveyed the room, then his hollow eyes found Billy, seeing him for the first time. Without a word, he fell back into one of only two chairs in the building. The sprung cushions coughed under his weight. "Yeah," said Billy. "Why don't you sit…?"

Danny didn't respond. He seemed hollow. Like someone had opened him up and scooped out everything that made him Danny.

This isn't fair, Billy thought. *He's supposed to be the sober one. I can't handle this shit right now.* He said, instead, "Wow, you're really fucked. You need a beer."

More substances! That's what was called for. Two ice cold beers from the mini fridge.

He handed one to Danny, who then held the top to his lips but did nothing further. Billy reached over and twisted the cap off the bottle, then returned the vessel to Danny's mouth.

Great. Catatonics are the worst. Boring motherfuckers… Billy flopped down on the other chair, tried to be nonchalant. "So…? What's new?"

Danny groaned like a zombie, "Blood..."

Billy waited for a follow-up. None came. "In general? You need some? You got some to sell?"

Danny let out a scream of anguish that even seemed to startle the mechanical people. He hurled the beer bottle into the distant darkness where it exploded. "There was blood everywhere! She killed them!"

Then Danny was on his feet, pacing in a tight circle around the chair. "She killed him right in front of me!"

"Whoa, whoa, there, kemosabe. You're way ahead of me. Who killed whom?"

"Laura!"

Billy blinked, trying to comprehend the syllables. *Laura? Laura who? Laura... oh fuck.* "Wait a minute..."

"Just killed him in front of me."

"Laura Baxter? The sleeping chick?"

"You know what's weird about people dying?"

The question derailed Billy's alarmed train of thought. "A lot of things," he answered.

"That's just it. Nothing was weird at all. It was just matter of fact." Danny held his hands out in front of him, as if acting something out with invisible dolls. "She killed them. And they just... died. They just stopped being alive. She... ended their lives. And then they were just dead. Not people any more. Just dead... things on the floor."

Billy didn't say anything for a long time. Finally, he broke the silence, "I'm gonna get you another beer."

IT WAS BARELY 8:30 in the morning. Christine had already *almost* been late to work thanks to the lousy street closure on Eleventh Ave. Then she couldn't find a place to park, as usual. And god forbid Murray Landis of Landis Furnishings provide parking for any of the employees. But the parking lot was for customers. Murray made that clear. There was even a little tin sign out back. "Customers Only."

She raced in. Nobody had made coffee, because why would Jenny get off her fat ass and do anything to help the rest of the "team?"

Team. There's a joke and a half. And now this.

Some strange woman came in off the street, made herself all too comfortable, and now she wouldn't wake up.

"I tried to wake her up," Christine said to Murray. "But she just *won't*."

"Is she on something?"

"You heard me say she didn't wake up, right? Which means she didn't tell me."

"Well we can't have a bunch of homeless people using this place as a flop house."

"It's one person. Not a bunch."

"You got to pay more attention to what's going on in your department."

"It's your store, Murray."

"And you're the Assistant Manager, Christine."

"Not according to my paycheck."

Murray didn't like to swear, so he didn't. But he *thought* really hard at her as he followed Christine to Section 5A, King and Queen Pillow Top Adjustables. In one of the more reasonably-priced models, there was a young woman, blonde, dirty, curled up in a big coat, sound asleep. She even had a little smile on her face, comfortable and safe.

"Miss?" said Murray, trying to rouse her without touching her. (Murray was less concerned with "catching something" than he was a

lawsuit for sexual assault or something. Hope-
fully, Christine would vouch for him.) "Miss?"
he said again when the non-physical touching
failed to work. Finally, he reached out with an
index finger and poked the girl's shoulder, gently, barely making an impression on the coat
sleeve.

"Young lady? You have to wake up."

When there was no response, Murray gave
Christine a quick glance, then rudely shoved at the
girl's arm. "Miss?"

"Maybe she's dead," said Christine, and Murray
couldn't tell if she was joking or not. He opted for
"not."

"She's not dead," he said, more to himself than
Christine. "Go get Rudy in Sporting Goods." She
just stared at him. "He used to be a paramedic..."

"I think he was a para*legal*—"

"Just go!"

WHILE DANNY WAS MID-STORY, Billy got up and
started pacing too. They passed each other, back
and forth in the center of the room, never even
saying "bread-and-butter," just talking and listening. When he finished, Danny collapsed back into
the chair, as if the story was the only thing keeping
him upright and on his feet.

Billy kept pacing. He was coming down, getting
jittery. The story he'd just heard was, was... "Well,
Danny that's the craziest fucking story I've ever
heard."

Danny just nodded.

"But there is a chick involved, so of course it's
true. No one will ever accuse you of a lack of imagi-
nation. Certainly not in the women you choose.

And so quick, too. Is Denise's side of the bed even cool yet?"

Assuming that was rhetorical, Danny didn't answer. "It's funny-"

"Yep, hilarious."

"No… as I've been telling you the story I realized something."

Billy waited. It was a long pause. Then:

"I love her."

Billy Dornboss rolled his eyes so hard, he saw the roots of his hair. "Of course, you do."

"No, I mean I *really* love her…"

"I mean really of course! You wouldn't be the all-day sucker you are if you didn't. Go from the cheater to the killer. At least it's more than a lateral move."

But Danny wasn't listening. They were talking over each other. "—like I've never loved anyone else. That's what been wrong with me… I think I've *always* loved her… From that first day I saw her."

"Last month?"

"When we were kids!"

"Oh, yeah, that bit." Billy finished his third beer. His stash of crystal was calling to him.

"Danny, buddy, light of my loins, she killed at least two people that you know about—she tried to kill *you*."

Danny sat up then, his head shaking in defiant denial. "No, she didn't."

"You just said she did!"

"She hasn't killed anyone." Danny fixed his friend with his most intense look yet. There had been things clawing at the back of his brain. Things he saw in dreams. That face. That worm-white face and its black eyes. Thumping its head against the padded walls of his cell. "Byron Volpe killed those people."

Billy didn't say anything right away. He just nodded. Danny was bye-bye now. "Sure, makes perfect sense."

Danny's eyes were crazed. "He's a *mesmerist*."

Billy put up his hands, palms out. "Hey, I'm cool with the theory. Volpe killed those people. But, see? I'm a drug addict, dude. I don't see how you're going to convince anyone of that who isn't."

"I messed up…"

"Yep."

"I let her down."

"No…"

"I have to go back to her. I have to help her… I caused this. This is my fault."

"Danny, for once in your fucking life, listen to me. You know I'm the last person to tell *anyone* to go to the police, but I don't think you have any other options here. You've got to go to them— *Danny, yes*, you have to go to them and tell them what happened. Tell 'em you had nothing to do— you didn't kill those people. Tell 'em that it was Sleeping fucking Beauty."

"I can't do that, I can't betray her. This is my fault."

"Are you taking crazy medicine, man? They're gonna lock you up you do that. What are they gonna do to *her*? Huh? She'll just go back to sleep anyway. She's already got her life sentence."

There was a look in Danny's eyes that Billy recognized from his many stays in rehab. It was a look of obsessive guilt, the consuming drive of a junkie. Danny's junk of choice was damaged women. He didn't need drugs to be who he was.

"I've got to set her free then," Danny said. "Free from Volpe."

And Billy knew there was no arguing with him.

Still: "What are you going to do? Danny? What are you gonna fucking do, man?"

Without turning back, Danny threw on his hoodie and went for the door. "Billy, if they catch me, you're not involved."

"No shit."

"I was never here."

"If only."

"Take it easy."

"Yeah," Billy said, watching his friend slouch off towards oblivion. "You too."

WHEN HER EYES FINALLY OPENED, Laura found that she was still in Dannyland. The nice soft bed he'd made for her had been perfect, but now there were strangers around her, telling her that she had to go. And they were right. She had to find Danny.

"I don't know who Danny is," said the woman with the ponytail and dark circles under her eyes. "But if I see him, I'll tell him you were here."

"Me too," said the big man in the uniform and the badge. He had a beard and he seemed nice too. Everyone in Dannyland was nice.

They helped her out the door and she was back on the sidewalk. Cars and big trucks went by. It was still loud and bright. Danny had to be close.

"Home," she said to the ponytail woman. "I have to go home... I don't know where it is. It's a building with lots of rooms."

But the ponytail lady patted her hand and then the bearded man patted her head. Like she was a dog or something. "Look sweetie, there's a homeless shelter about ten blocks East of here. Go get yourself a good night's rest, okay?"

"Just do yourself a favor," said the bearded man with the yellow badge, "and don't come back here."

"Okay," Laura said. She didn't *want* to go back there. This was boring. "Danny?" she called. Why couldn't he hear her?

"Hey there, sweetie," said a voice from behind her. The voice smelled bad and so did the man it belonged to. He had on sunglasses and had thinning black hair. He smelled like... hospital.

"Hi," she said to him. If he lived in Dannyland, he had to be nice. "Do you know where Danny is?"

The man smiled and showed all of his teeth. He had big gums. "I can be Danny if you like."

Laura frowned. That didn't make any sense. He wasn't Danny and couldn't *be* Danny. "Are you from Hospital?"

The stranger looked confused. He had one hand in his pants pocket, gripping something. "Hospital?" He took a step closer. "No... but I'm definitely what the doctor ordered."

"The doctor sent you?" she asked, suddenly alarmed. "What doctor? Corso? Not Bhyle, right? Not Bhyle?"

And then the stranger took a step back, looking at her like she was some kind of wild animal. "Are you retarded or something?"

Laura gasped. "No! I'm very smart. I'm just... ignorant... Look, do you know Danny? I can't find him."

The stranger's demeanor changed again to friendly, and he moved closer, running his fingers down the sleeves of Danny's big coat. "Maybe we can find him together. You are a pretty thing. You could use some new clothes though, don't you think? I could help you out."

Dannyland people passed them on the sidewalk. Nobody looked in their direction. Nobody cared.

The stranger's fingers hovered over the hollow of her throat. They shook a little as he opened up her coat to see what was beneath.

Blood.

That was what was beneath.

Blood had plastered the nightgown to the breasts he'd expected to see. His excitement vanished in panic. "What the hell? What have you done?"

Laura pulled away from him, closing the coat around herself, ashamed and angry.

The stranger's eyes were wide. "What's wrong with you?"

Laura felt her lips curl into a snarl. "*Nothing's* wrong with me! Get away from me! You're mean!"

She turned away from the man and hurried down the sidewalk. She didn't know where she was going. Just *forward*. The stranger didn't chase her or anything. Nobody said anything to her. At the end of the block was another road. There were cars coming both ways and she didn't know how to get across. She didn't know if there was anything to cross *for*.

She felt sleepy again. She was frustrated and tired and getting hot in the coat and *where was Danny*?

There was a little staircase leading to a building. The stairs were low and perfect for sitting. She was so tired. "Danny!" she called, but then Sleep took her and Dannyland faded away.

SOMETIME LATER, a patrol car showed up to answer a call about a vagrant sleeping on an apartment stoop. The description was "young, Caucasian, female."

Officers Bottoms and Combs made sure their bodycams were on. They didn't need another investigation on their hands.

Dispatch called just as they got the sleeping girl into the back seat. Laura Baxter, this missing sleepwalking patient, was to be returned to the Hamilton-Hart Hospital. Combs radioed in and reported that they were on the way.

"Nothing like a nice easy day, eh Tim?" he said to Bottoms.

AT THAT EXACT MOMENT, in a pawnshop in The Docks, Danny leaned on the glass cabinet, looking over a variety of handguns.

CHAPTER 17

Hanging above the nurse's station on the eleventh floor of the Hamilton-Hart Hospital was a little sign, a cartoon of a nurse, her scrubs stained with god-knew what, each hand burdened with stacks of meds and bedpans, looking exhausted, cheeks red and puffed out, but with a slight smile. The bold balloon letters stacked to her right read: "Nurses: Full-Time, Full-Blown, Under-Paid And Appreciated." In the two years she'd worked there, Sarah had never heard a single doctor acknowledge the sign. She doubted it even registered on their egos.

Though Sarah Laine was only twenty-five, she'd seen plenty during "full-time, full-blown, under-paid and appreciated" career. The worst cases always involved kids. Abuse, drugs, rape, *babies*. But in jobs such as these, one learns to compartmentalize. You can't bring the tragedy home with you. Sometimes, you can't even sit with it while it's present.

In two years, she'd been groped and otherwise assaulted, insulted, called slurs, received face-to-face death threats—"And that's just from the doctors!" the nurses would all joke, but never laugh—

coma patients who would never wake up, hooked to machines to keep the bodies alive, whatever had been inside had died long ago, but the families couldn't face it. Sometimes, Sarah thought, *hope* was the cruelest emotion God could have created.

To say that, ordinarily, Sarah Laine was unflappable would be an understatement. She was often the calm in the storm that could often be the hospital night shift.

But tonight, with a literal storm raging outside, and a shift that was already down two due to a stomach flu going around, and cops coming and going because of the return of the kidnapped sleeping woman—Sarah's nerves were already frayed when it came time to feed the patients. Particularly one patient: Byron motherfucking Volpe.

"First, do no harm." Hippocrates never met Byron Volpe.

She'd seen him without his hood, of course. She'd had to oversee his cleaning, shaving, but always when he was sedated. And even then, laid out on the floor, getting hosed off like a zoo animal, they kept his wrists shackled. And *always*, gauze was taped over his eyes. Lest he wake up and look at you.

"Whatever you do, don't look at him." That was the wise council of Dr. Corso. His *only* council. Because, like every other doctor in every other hospital, Dr. Corso didn't have to deal with his patients' actual daily needs.

Normally, the senior nurse, Helen, took care of the nightly feedings. If you called Helen a "battle axe," she'd take it as a compliment. Bully patients didn't stand a chance with Helen. Either she'd kill you with kindness or remind you that she alone controlled your pain medication.

Tonight, Helen was at home with a vomiting

grandchild. It was up to Sarah to get everyone fed. Volpe included.

For a change, Volpe stood motionless in the center of his room, instead of slamming his head into the wall, which was usually his custom. She got the door open and wheeled in his tray. It would be cold. She intentionally fed him last. She hated even being in the same building as this scary motherfucker.

He was at least a foot-and-a-half taller than she, and Sarah had to stand on tip-toe to push up his hood, just enough to expose his nose and mouth. As the air hit his face, Volpe *sniffed* at her. A long, deliberate, taunting sniff, angling his face at her.

Acid reflux sat boiling at the back of her throat, making her want to chatter her teeth. Volpe hadn't been bathed in some time and seemed to be aware at how offensive his own odor was. Obviously, he enjoyed it.

Volpe's gag looked like a steampunk sink stopper. A combination bondage-mask and Hannibal Lecter get-up. The center was perfectly round, like a plug, and opened like a porthole. Even with gloves, she didn't want to touch it, or get her fingers that close to his mouth.

When his mouth was freed, Volpe wagged his tongue through the round opening, slurping at her, licking at the scent of her in the air, gray like a flatworm.

You've had to do worse, Sarah, she told herself, and used the voice of her grandmother to further shame and motivate. All they fed Volpe at night was creamed corn. Really, they should just shove a funnel in his mouth and smoothie him to death, but... *First Do No Harm*. Gag reflex fully engaged, Sarah spooned up some of the nauseating yellow porridge and used the utensil to fight the writhing tongue, forcing it back into the glistening mouth.

There was a sudden ringing in the back of her head. The sight of the mouth—lips flapping through a mess of corn and saliva—made her stomach drop. *Fuck this fuck this fuck this*—Sarah dropped the tray to the ground and backed away, hands up in defeat. Pulling the cart out with her, she slammed the door shut. Let an orderly clean that shit up. Or let Volpe just sit in it. She didn't give one good goddamn. She was *done* for the night.

ALONE AGAIN, Volpe worked his head around until the hood rode his forehead like an ill-fitting hat. He smiled at the closed door, knowing that if he let the worms out, they could find young Nurse Sarah wherever she was, but it was easier to just lock eyes and *tell her* what he wanted her to do. No, not *easier*. Just *more fun*.

He didn't care about the mess on his face. He was a god. Gods can have corn on their faces.

What he *did* care about—the bit that was really making him laugh, rather than the mere torment of a young female—was that he'd *finally* worked a hole in the seam of his left restraining glove. He got three fingers free.

Tick, tick, tick.

ACROSS THE STREET from the rear of the Hamilton-Hart Hospital, Danny has plastered himself against the wall of the parking lot, like an escaped fugitive, waiting for the searchlight and the screws to find him. His head was pounding. He was exhausted, definitely dehydrated. Severe insomnia often results in impaired thinking, slurred speech. Hallucination.

The gun in the pocket of his hoodie was a revolver. He remembered the pawn shop guy saying it was a thirty-something. .38? .39?— whatever. He also bought six bullets and they fit perfectly in the chamber. All he had to do was get up close to Volpe and *pop*.

Or *pow*. Whatever.

Danny had anticipating seeing Lewis, the big Black security guard, but at the rear entrance was a single uniformed cop, his back to the street. Danny moved carefully across the street, taking advantage of the shadows cast by the rumbling storm clouds above. The rain refused to break, but the thunder and the lighting crashed and seemed to follow Danny from his apartment to the Hospital. Just waiting until the right moment to ruin his plans.

Feeling only slightly ridiculous, Danny slipped through the gate and crouched down behind a parked car. He could hear the cop's *walkie* chirp.

"Go for Doucette," Danny heard the cop say.

Another *chirp*: "*Positive ID on sleeping kidnap victim Laura Baxter. She's being returned to Hamilton-Hart… Over.*"

Officer Doucette responded while walking: "What's my status, over?" and then disappeared around the corner, giving Danny a free path towards entry. He didn't know if they were looking for him—or even who *they* were. But he had his mission.

Gathering his will, Danny gripped the gun in his pocket in the hopes of finding excess bravery somewhere in there with the bullets. He took a

deep breath and let it out, the got to his feet. And
screamed:

"Jesus fucking Christ!"

Right into the face of the priest who'd startled
him by minding his own business there in the
darkness.

"I'm terribly sorry," sputtered the priest. Big
fella. Big ol' priest. In black with the white square
collar and everything. "I never meant to startle
you."

That's when Danny saw the cigarette between
the man's fingers, and the guilty look on the man's
face as he tried to hide it. "We all sin in different
ways," said the priest.

"I'll go do mine," Danny said. For no particular
reason. His brain was so tired.

Between visits to Billy and then Laura, Danny
had no problem navigating the labyrinthine corridors of the hospital. He knew it was shift-change
and therefore his chances of getting in and out
without making too much of a scene were good,
but only if he moved fast.

"Excuse me..." came a gruff voice behind him.
"Visiting hours are over."

Goddamn it.

Danny tossed on his disarming smile, but his
face didn't really want to work. "Hi. Evening," he
said to Chief of Security Malcolm Lewis. They were
old friends, right?

Lewis stared at Danny's weirdly contorted face.
"I know you, don't I?

"Yeah! Yes, my grandmother was here and–"

"Uh uh," Lewis said. "Your Grandmother? No,
not on my floor. Do you have some ID?"

*Yessir, in the same pocket as my brand new gun!
Shitshitshit—*

The elevator *dinged* and vomited out a half

dozen angry-looking men and women in lab coats. At the front of the pack was a man who wore his authority and beard for the same effect. Danny recognized the charging bull immediately: Dr. Egon Bhyle. There was a good chance that Bhyle would *not* recognize him. Men like Bhyle didn't "do" faces. Regardless, Danny ducked his head down.

"You stay right here," Lewis told him, then turned to head off the stampede. "Excuse me… can I help you?"

Bhyle didn't even look at Lewis, just shoved a piece of paper in his face. "Dr. Egon Bhyle. Here to pick up my patient, Laura Baxter. Now if you'll be so good as to step aside."

"Bhyle? Fine. But they just got her in. Need to check with Dr. Corso to make sure she can be moved again."

"*I* am her doctor, *not* Corso," puffed Bhyle.

Lewis was not in the mood.

Danny slipped away, letting the security guard handle the flock of doctors. He was a knight and there was a dragon to slay.

The psycho wing of eleven was nearly deserted. A clumsy robot weedled into a room to take stats and freak out a patient. Danny waited until it trundled out again and kept it between him and the nurses' station. There was only one nurse on the floor, it seemed—*thank you shift change*—and she looked exhausted and harassed. Had she been crying?

One princess at a time, Sir Asshole.

The young nurse left the station, vanished around a corner. As the robot resumed its duties, Danny resumed normal speed. The nurse had left her keys on the desk. One of them *must* open Volpe's vault.

Under his hood, Volpe was very much awake and very much alert. Suddenly, he was also very happy.

"She's back," he said to no one.

He stretched his neck. He stretched his back. He let his shoulder muscles contract, relax, contract again, and he worked at the hole in his leather gauntlet. Then he sent his thoughts out:

Laura… you came back to me.

No. Not quite. Yes, she was asleep, but she wasn't in his realm.

Volpe thought for a moment. Should he release the worms?

Laura… Laura…? I can see you, he lied. He felt her presence. She was back in her bed. Just next door. So close. So near. So… so fucking what? How was she evading his grasp?

Volpe felt anger swirl in him. He loved it. He loved the way it burned and turned his thoughts from gray to red.

LAURA!

She was… *hiding* from him. It made him laugh. It had been so long since he'd been challenged.

Volpe laughed and it was loud and deep and sounded like an oncoming train. He didn't even hear Danny open the door behind him.

But, oh… he *felt* it.

Gun in hand, Sir Danny walked into the dragon's den. The evil sorcerer was right where he'd been left, semi-crucified, tethered to his cell in unbreakable bonds. With trickery his only weapon. Danny swallowed hard, and Volpe seemed to take notice.

Twisting his neck in a strange way, Volpe's head lolled on his shoulders, turning—impossibly—to face Danny. He'd worked the hood back, just above the bridge of his nose. Clamping his jaws, he was able to bite through the plug of metal and rubber that had held his mouth open but unspeaking. He spit the remains at Danny's feet. Finally, the sorcerer was free to speak.

"Welcome," he said to the knight in the doorway. "I see the clock has run down. The ticking is about to stop. A willing partner for our Danse Macabre."

Sir Danny's heart was racing, his breath coming out in sharp pants. Pulling the gun from his pocket, the hammer caught on the fabric, but just for half a second. A small fumble. Nothing more. Weapon drawn, Danny took a step closer to the adversary. To show he was serious, he thumbed back the hammer.

At the sound, Volpe seemed to shudder in obscene anticipation. "The Clouded Man approaches... weapon in hand... This is really much less Shakespearean and more Hugh B. Cave don't you think?"

(*Born in 1910*, Danny's brain recited, *this author of horror and speculative fiction published his last novel, Serpents in the Sun, in 2011.*)

"Shut up," was all Danny could think to say.

"We really need to elevate your reading habits. Have you ever read *Great Expectations*? Wonderful book! You really should think of me more like Magwitch. Your benefactor."

"Shut *up!*" Danny shouted again, the anger making him bolder. He took another step closer to Volpe, the barrel leveled at the sorcerer's head.

But the serpent-speak continued to hiss out from the glistening mouth full of too many white and even teeth. "You've come to free Sleeping Beauty," Volpe chuckled. "My dear Pip, a kiss isn't going to do it. She's an orphan with an orphan's disease. She's not going to be fixed. She's mine only. I have had her so many times in those dark dreams we share." Again, that horrible, triumphant laugh meant to mock and draw blood. "A word of advice for the future-"

"I'm done listening." Danny's finger tensed on the trigger. *I'm going to do it—now!*

But Volpe finished: "Never assume."

Danny heard a *rip* as Volpe's hand came free of the canvas restraint and slapped him across the head. The gun screamed and performed its function, but the bullet went nowhere important. Danny and the gun flew in opposite directions.

Blurred vision and a throbbing skull, that was Danny's universe. He could hear the sound of more canvas ripping, of the sorcerer freeing himself entirely, but he was helpless to move. His body refused to obey his agonized brain's commands.

Far off in the distance, he heard a familiar voice: "Freeze right there! Move again and you'll be talking to Jesus!"

Who was the voice talking to? The knight or the sorcerer?

Malcolm Lewis, head of security, took a tentative step into the room, gun oscillating between Danny and Volpe. The enormous, monstrous patient had freed himself.

"I said, don't move!" the guard repeated.

Then Volpe removed his hood.

"Don't move!"

Volpe stood upright before the guard, before the fallen knight. He smiled so very widely. "I just wanted to thank you. He was going to hurt me."

His hand shaking, Lewis had trouble keeping

the gun steady. *Those fucking eyes of his...* "No, you don't!" the guard shouted, throwing a hand over his eyes. "Somebody come help me!"

The sound of feet—small feet—running down the hallway towards them. Volpe smiled.

He let the worms out.

He heard Nurse Sarah's angry voice. "What is going on?" The last word dried up in her mouth as she locked eyes with Volpe and the worms found their way in.

Volpe never lost his smile. "Nothing really..."

The worms showed her spinning mechanical eyes. They showed her the things that were already in her brain and that just needed to be let out. Nothing was her fault. She was just a puppet.

Dance, puppet. Dance, poppet.

Volpe and his worms made a spider-web of electricity and rode the synapses of her brain.

He spoke the magic chant. Just one simple word:

"Tick, Tick, Tick, Tick, Tick!"

"Sarah, you gotta call 911!" said Lewis, his eyes still shielded. (As if *that* could protect him from the worms.) "Tell them—"

Nurse Sarah didn't let him finish. The scalpel she didn't know she'd been holding in her hand flashed in the light just as it plunged into Lewis' jugular vein. The guard's throat exploded.

Blood showered the room, spraying Danny, spraying Nurse Sarah. Nurse Sarah stabbed the guard again, and didn't even blink when the gore showered her face. In fact, she seemed to find the color quite fascinating. It glistened in the fluorescent light. Rubies... she was coated in rubies.

The sorcerer turned to the fallen knight. "And now, for you," he whispered.

Volpe's eyes drilled deep into Danny's nervous

system. Casually, with the strength of his will, he hurled the puppet from the room. Danny hit the cart headfirst. Body, instruments, and utensils, all slammed into the opposite wall. The knight fell into unconsciousness.

Shedding the last of his restraints, Volpe the god felt good to finally stretch his legs. He stepped over the body of the guard, past the little nurse who was no longer among the rational.

With a contented sigh, Volpe crouched over the fallen knight and began to search his pockets. His princess was just a few feet away. His foes have been vanquished. But there was so much more fun to be had. Now, who was this errant knight anyway?

Bus pass, wallet, ID. Daniel Sloan. Little black book. A little sheaf of crumpled papers, all talking about Byron Volpe. Why look, a picture of the old bookstore where Volpe used to play-

Volpe chuckled to himself and flipped through Danny's little address book. Names, addresses, wait…

"Dornboss."

That name struck Volpe as familiar. Had he heard it somewhere? Maybe in Danny's brain? Wait… Dornboss. He'd been a neighbor, hadn't he?

So that's where this knight errant came from. That was the connection.

It was time to gather the princess and prepare a welcoming ceremony in her honor. Maybe "Dornboss" would be useful. As for the knight, as for Daniel Sloan…

Volpe felt a tug at the leg of his pajama pants. Looking down at the young nurse, who looked up at him like a dog seeking approval, Volpe smiled and patted her head. Then they locked eyes and exchanged a thousand thousand thoughts.

Volpe turned and left her there, to pick through the overturned medical supplies until she found surgical thread and a very long needle. What fun she could have with this needle and this thread.

There was even someone to play with...

CHAPTER 18

IT TOOK NO TIME AT ALL TO CONVINCE DR. BHYLE AND his staff to take their own lives. No time at all. They *wanted* to cut their own throats. Dr. Bhyle was happy to take a long hypodermic needle and shove it up through his soft palate and into his nasal cavity. It only took a couple of firm taps to stab it into his brain. For all his accomplishments and successes, virtuesand talents, nothing came as close to greatness than what he'd just achieved.

That was his last thought before the needle pierced his brain.

Volpe smiled.

Stepping over the fallen bodies, Volpe moved to Laura. He'd caught them in mid-transfer so she was free of wires, plugs, tubes. Free for him.

He gathered her into her arms, left behind one last little present for the curious, and carried her from the hospital.

Outside, Volpe found a priest loitering in the parking lot. The old man smiled guiltily at the sight, hastily hiding a small hip flask. "Just tending to the sick," he explained.

The giant carrying the unconscious young girl

didn't seem the least bit out of the ordinary to Father Donnelly. The worms made sure of that.

"I need your car," said Volpe. And the priest nodded. "But first, I need your clothing."

"Yes, of course," said the Father, unbuttoning his shirt, letting the plastic collar spring free. "My son," he added.

Volpe donned the garb of the holy man and waited for his return. Father Donnelly sat naked in the driver's seat, waiting for instruction.

"Stop breathing," Volpe said. And the priest obeyed. Volpe opened the car door and let the dead priest tumble onto the pavement. Gently, he laid Laura across the back seat, then assumed his place behind the wheel, while humming tunelessly to himself, content and even proud of what he'd just accomplished. "All good things come to those who wait," he said. "Aphorisms are true."

He felt no need to rush. The celebration was necessary and there was still a venue to consider. Out of curiosity, Volpe popped open the Caddy's glove compartment and sorted through the contents. Warranty, insurance card, all registered to the priest's diocese. *What's this?*

A full-color glossy pamphlet with glowing crosses and doves in the margins, announcing an event: "Our Lady of the Sacred Heart 6th Autumn Classical Recital."

Two very beautiful young girls graced the photo beneath the banner. One light of hair, one dark. Posing with their instruments. The blonde played viola, the brunette the cello. There was nothing sexual about the photo, but Volpe's body responded anyway. Saliva filled his mouth. He pictured the girls heralding the transformation of his Sleeping Beauty into an Eternal Angel.

In the upper left corner, the priest had scrawled

in blue pen ink: "Pick up girls at 10:00 PM." There was even an address.

What a helpful old man he'd been.

Volpe put the car into gear and drove away, leaving the corpse of the helpful old man in the street.

CHAPTER 19

Lighting flashed over the Hamilton-Hart Hospital. Danny woke up to a nightmare.

A piercing alarm filled the halls, accompanied by an alert flashing red, then blackness. The storm had knocked out the lights. Or, more probably, Volpe. The lightning illuminated the room, gave him a flash of horror that lingered on his eyes in afterimage.

He'd been lying face-down in a puddle of someone else's blood. There was a needle in his arm, draining *his* blood into a bag. Across from him, in Volpe's former cell, the young nurse sat on the guard's chest. She had a long suture needle in her hand. She was sewing up the guard's eyes. As if sensing Danny's eyes, she turned to him to smile. It was difficult—she'd sewn her lips shut. Her lidless eyes were wide but Danny didn't know what she saw.

Whatever Volpe told her to see.

Tearing the needle from his arm, he scrambled away from her, his wound weeping. The nurse didn't pursue. The blood-slick floor made it difficult for his feet to find purchase, but finally he was upright, head pounding. He could feel blood dripping down his collar behind his ear. He didn't care. He had to find Laura before Volpe—

How long had he been unconscious?

Whirling, his feet slid, almost toppling him again. His address book—a bloody thumbprint by Billy's address—and something else. The printout about the Volpe Bookstore.

Head pounding, Danny couldn't think. The distance between him and Laura's room seemed endless, yet he managed to cover it in just a few strides, only to find even more horror inside.

Volpe had left no survivors. Danny's misfiring brain managed to recognize each member of Bhyle's team—some had stabbed their eyes out before slitting their own throats. The syringe jutting from Bhyle's open mouth made Danny think of a walrus. (*What is "Goo Goo Ga-Joob?" No, seriously, what is it?*)

Laura's bed was empty. Only bloody handprints on the sheets and a bloodstained teddy bear left behind on her pillow, like a changeling.

Laura.

Volpe had her. But he'd left behind clues. *Deliberately?* Where would he take her?

The bookstore or to Billy's? What would he even want with Billy?

Danny's body decided not to wait for his brain. The feet began moving. He wondered where they'd take him.

Who was Cesar the Somnambulist?

No matter how many times they played, Darcy never tired of the piece. In her head, she heard the lyrics:

She could even remember the lyricist: Cecil Spring-Rice. She liked that. It sounded like a healthy meal. "Thaxted" by Gustav Holst for his *Jupiter Suite*. She never really knew what "Thaxted" meant and always intended to Google it. But then she'd get lost in the piece.

Ave Maria, Bach's various pieces, they bored her so easily. But not *Jupiter*. It sounded so wonderful in the empty Conservatory Hall. She always loved it when it was just the two of them and the music. The rest of the world just fell away like a dream.

The piece came to its end. Darcy and Miranda smiled at each other. Darcy over her Cello, Miranda and her Viola. It *almost* rhymed.

The two girls almost rhymed too. Darcy was brunette, Miranda almost Nordic blonde. Their dresses complimented each other in shades of red—Darcy dark crimson, Miranda almost pink. They looked like pre-Raphaelite angels. At least, that was the look Father Donnelly had chosen for them for the concert tonight. He'd had... specific ideas about the whole thing.

The two girls had both recently turned 20—their birthdays so close together, they were almost twins, Snow White and Rose Red—but appeared so much younger in their fancy costumes.

Our Lady of the Sacred Heart 6th Autumn Classical Recital. It was such a big deal for Father Donnelly. Rich parishioners were sure to attend. Which would be a good thing. Money was running out. The lawsuit that Darcy wasn't supposed to know about had almost wiped out the district.

Father Donnelly would be there soon to pick them up. The two young women wiped down their instruments with soft polish cloths, gently packed the heavy instruments away into their velvet-lined cases. They giggled at the absurdity of the two petite women in near-Victorian garb lugging instrument cases the size of steamer trunks out to the parking lot.

Outside, they hear a car pull up. Miranda smiled. Darcy checked and indicated with a forefinger against her own incisors that Miranda had lipstick on her teeth.

"Thanks," said Miranda. "I'll see if that's our ride."

"I'll finish locking up," said Darcy.

Courteously, Darcy packed up the two folding chairs and returned them to their stacks. Never leave a mess for others to clean up, she'd been taught. Turning out the lights, she was struck by how cavernous the place could be even in the early evening. Especially when she was all alone.

Of course, she wasn't all alone. She was with—

Darcy stopped and listened to the quiet? "Miranda?"

Her only response was her distant echo.

Dragging the cello case behind her, Darcy nearly killed herself on the stairs. She called for Miranda again, and again got no response.

Bursting through the rear door, she saw Miranda almost immediately. Illuminated by the bright headlights of a black Cadillac. On all fours on the ground.

"What are you doing?"

But Miranda didn't answer. Her shoulders hitched like she was sobbing. Darcy came around. "What's wrong?" Miranda looked up at her. A blindfold of black cloth was wrapped around her eyes. Darcy ran to her side and crouched down, touching the girl's ivory shoulder. "What is it? What happened? What—"

The shadows grew a body with bright red-black eyes glaring out of a too-white face.

Darcy wanted to scream but knew if she opened her mouth the worms would get in.

Her body quivered, fighting sobs. Fighting what the worms wanted her to do.

She said to the shadow in her head: "No! Please take your eyes off me. Please stop!"

Deep, deep inside Darcy's mind, something shattered. As Miranda was no longer Miranda, Darcy was no longer Darcy. The two girls were as hollow and empty as their instruments.

And could be played just as beautifully.

Detective Garrett had lost track of how many bloodbaths he'd seen that week. How many more mutilated bodies would he have to gag over before this was done?

Why couldn't it just be a couple of junkies on a bender? Why couldn't it be a couple of mobsters? Why did it have to be this weird serial killer shit?

Why couldn't he have been one of those cops who'd never had to pull his gun? Why did he get all the fucked up cases?

Volpe was out there somewhere. So was Daniel Sloan, killer of Det. Hank Conroy. Somewhere in the middle was half-a-vegetable in a porn star's body. How they all connected, Garrett had no idea, and quite frankly he didn't give a shit anymore. He was *done*.

Tonight he would either put an end to this bull-shit, or he'd eat his goddamned gun.

CHAPTER 20

The Cadillac oozed around the corner like a black worm, entering the area known as The Docks. Behind the wheel, Volpe hummed his tuneless tune. He looked into the rearview mirror and smiled at the two girls in the backseat, both blindfolded and obedient. Quiet, demure. Like nice young ladies should be. Next to him in the passenger seat, the sleeping angel, Laura, continued to doze, unaware of all. She was still somewhere Volpe couldn't quite reach, but it didn't bother him. All in good time.

It wasn't difficult to locate Dornboss's building. It was the only one for blocks with interior lights on. Every other squat flat warehouse sat quiet and dark beneath its security lights warning off no one in particular.

Volpe parked the Caddy, leaving his little entourage where they were. As a little joke, he cracked the windows and left the radio on. Not one of the three was in any condition to listen, but there was no sense in letting them suffer. Not yet anyway.

Inside the building, light flickered erratically, and almost seemed to line up to the beat of the pulsing musical noise spilling out of every broken window. Apparently Mr. Dornboss was "in the zone." Volpe smiled. He let the worms run free.

After a moment—much longer than Volpe expected, truth be told—the flickering stopped. A few seconds later, so did the music. Shadows passed the window, then Dornboss appeared, leaning unconcerned against the pane.

"Open up, William," Volpe said. "I've brought company."

Slowly, Billy Dornboss nodded, like one of his automatons. Then a grin broke across his face. With robotic movements, Billy extended both arms, hands curled into a fist. He made hydraulic noises with his mouth as he did so. The movement ended with two middle fingers erected especially for Byron Volpe. "Take your company," said Billy Dornboss, "and go fuck yourselves. You don't scare me, creep."

For the first time in forever, Volpe experienced surprise. "Open the door, William," he said, eyes black, voice commanding.

Dornboss laughed. It was ugly. Mocking. Offensive. Volpe stared at the unpleasant little man who was somehow defying him. The worms had no effect. Billy Dornboss was immune. Volpe could taste all the chemicals in the young man's brain, residue from a thousand thousand fixes. He'd made himself immune to outside madness.

As he closed the window, Billy waved and silently mouthed "bye-bye, fucker."

Ah well, Volpe thought. There's more than one way to get into a building.

And there's more than one way to get into somebody's head.

Across town, another shadow arrived at another darkened building. The sign above the door proclaimed "VOLPE'S RARE BOOKS." Beneath, the sign:

"The Ultra-Rare For Those of Discerning Tastes - Specializing In Magic, The Occult And The Unusual."

Danny wondered, *Where was the Oxford Comma, you pretentious jagoff?*

Danny's reflection stared back. With the hair slicked to his head from sweat and rain, hollowed eyes, he barely recognized himself. The reflection gaped at him while he stared into the darkness beyond. Somewhere inside this building would be a key to Volpe's connection to Laura. Or possibly where he would take her. Or something valuable, this much uncertainty he knew.

Old crime scene tape, no longer yellow, faded from sun and wind and time, hung limp from the door like discarded parade streamers. Plastered to the entrance was an old weathered notice:

"ENTRANCE IS FORBIDDEN BY ORDER OF THE DISTRICT ATTORNEY'S OFFICE." Heavy padlocks had been added as further deterrence.

Around the corner, Danny found a series of narrow windows, low to the ground. Easy enough to smash open. Less easy to squeeze through. Danny dropped down into the dark and into Volpe's Wonderland.

As it turned out, Volpe's Wonderland was a dark, moldy maze of books, shelves, boxes, files. Most of it still tagged with evidence cards. As if the investigation had stopped when they'd had enough evidence, and including the rest of this would just be overkill.

Danny used the light from his cell phone to find his way around. At some point in the past a pipe had burst, the ceiling dripped and water pooled on the floor. It smelled like how he imagined a mausoleum would smell. Or King Tut's Tomb.

Somewhere in the dark, something panicked and skittered, toppling a pile of newspapers. Fantastic. *Tonight on 'Hoarders,' the Satanist's basement and the giant rat of Sumatra. Of course, it's too dark to even see what the fucking thing was.*

Passing into another room, Danny found it dry and slightly more inhabitable. Maybe office space? The walls were lined with posters of Edwardian magicians: Herrmann the Great, Howard Thurston —*The Whirling Crystal Cage and Magical Production: Thurston Kellar's successor* the poster proclaimed, complete with little red devils surrounding an elegant lady trapped inside a smoky glass tube. Strangely, not a Houdini to be found.

A desk at one end of the room, stacked with books and papers. *The Art of Zdzisław Beksiński* turned to a page showing a nightmare hellscape of ash and flame. Beneath, a couple of ancient books on anatomy, complete with brightly colored diagrams of an eviscerated body. How-to before YouTube. Inevitably, a copy of *Paradise Lost*, the angels waging war in Heaven against the Angels of Hell.

The *skittering* again—behind him. This time accompanied by a rattling hiss. *Great, an asthmatic giant rat.* He flashed the light around. The closest thing he could find to a weapon was an old curtain rod. It had some heft to it, though, might even be iron. Maybe the giant rat had come from Faerie and would find the iron toxic.

The skittering noise has something else behind it, or maybe accompanying it. Danny strained to listen, to separate the sounds of his footsteps from the skittering, not to mention all the screaming going on in his brain, begging him to get the fuck out of that moldy basement and *not* find the source of the noise.

Stepping forward changed his perspective and he found on the wall, hidden by shadow, a weird printed tin clock. It looked vaguely familiar, like something Billy would be obsessed with.

That was it. Thomas Kuntz. The clockmaker and automaton artist from the mid 1800s. He was one of Billy's favorite artists and the one sure to send him into a rage when mentioned. Danny had seen this clock before in a book about Kuntz.

It was colorful and garish like a carnival piece, but somehow sinister. The twisted image of a man wearing a derby hat—or maybe it was a bowler—which housed the clock face. The man's face had sleepy eyes and heavy lids behind rimless glasses. The eyes covered housings for something, Danny remembered.

Despite the urgency of his quest to find Laura, he found his concussed brain fascinated by the clock. He watched his hand reach out to touch the side, feel the smooth tin for himself.

Something inside the clock's guts began to whirl and click. His touch had brought it to life. The sleepy eyes flipped up—just as he'd expected—revealing swirling hypno-disks—*look into my eyes*—while the clock hands spun in opposite orbits. The smiling mouth articulated like a ventriloquist dummy's, dropping down, revealing a message between the teeth, white written on black. It asked: "How long do you have to live?"

Then the mouth closed. Something behind it clicked, and again the jaw dropped open and gave him the answer:

"Not Long Now."

Then the room filled with *ticking*—as if the room itself were a clock. The ticking beat against his ear drums then right into his brain. "Stop!" he demanded, and beat his fist against the clock. He ripped the vile thing off the wall and hurled it away to crash into the darkness.

As the clock died, so did the ticking.

Danny took a second to compose himself. He saw what the clock had been hiding: a small metal ring hanging from a short length of chain that snaked into a hole in the wall. "Yeah, tick, tick, tick, yourself."

Danny pulled the chain and the wall slid open. Just a few inches, like a haunted house movie. There it was, Volpe's inner sanctum.

More shelves, more books, more stacks of detritus covered with dust and mildew. This particular collection had a more medical focus, charts and diagrams of the nervous system, the endocrine system, ancient medical instruments looked better-designed for the Inquisition than Johns Hopkins.

Another Thurston poster hung on one wall. Opposite, covering the entirety of the wall, a charming history of contagious diseases and their effects. Syphilis was present, of course, as was leprosy—can't have a disease party without leprosy. There was almost something gleeful about the poster and its miseries.

Christ, it smelled bad.

Disgusted, Danny ripped the poster from the wall. Doing so, he revealed a dark stain. Roughly the size of a person. Again, his hand moved without advanced warning, and he watched his fingers pick at the stain. The plaster was mush and pushed in with ease. The small hole created a bigger one, with nearly half the wall disintegrating.

Despite desperately not wanting to, Danny shined his light into the brand new hole.

The first thing his brain registered was the belt of the rotting lace dress.

He didn't look at the face and no one would have blamed him for the revulsion. Whoever the woman had been, judging from the rot and the stench, she'd been in that wall for a long time. There was still plenty of flesh on the staring, screaming face. Although one side had been completely... *eaten* away.

HSSSSS! The giant rat snarled at clawed at him, protecting its nest and food supply. Biggest goddamned rat Danny had ever seen outside of his nightmares. The thing hissed and spit and then vanished back into the wall. At least it confirmed the source of the *skittering*. Ozzy the Rat Possum.

Danny took two quick steps back. Then something hard and metal was jammed behind his ear. He heard the distinct clicking of a revolver's hammer being thumbed back.

"Freeze," said the gun's owner, barely contained rage hissing through his teeth. "Don't you *fucking* move!"

Danny's body slipped back into autopilot and he started to turn towards his latest attacker.

"I said don't move!"

Danny froze, felt a hand slap against his body then smooth down. He was being frisked, not assaulted. Not that the realization made him relax, especially not when he felt the cold handcuffs snap tight around his wrists.

A rough shove against his shoulder spun him around. Another bulldog cop, dark thinning hair, the face of a man who'd been given a dire diagnosis and was out of fucks to give.

"Detective Jeff Garrett," he said. "You and I are going to have a nice little chat."

Danny nodded in resignation. Maybe this was

for the best. He was way in over his head. "All right. I know what you think, but I didn't kill anybody."

"Sure," Garrett said, and gestured with his gun to the hole in the wall. "Who's that then?"

Danny didn't know what to say. "I've never even been here before."

"Where's your ID?"

"I swear it was in my pocket!"

"What's your name, then, kid?"

"Daniel Sloan."

Just then the cop's demeanor changed. He went from angry and harassed to angry and interested. "Oh, yeah?" he said, raising the gun to Danny's face. "Daniel Sloan? I've been looking for you. You and I are going to have a very meaningful conversation."

"Look, I didn't do anything. I swear. I need—"

"That's funny. You know why that's funny? Because there's still the blood of a dead cop *all over* the floor of your apartment."

"I swear I didn't kill him."

Garrett got very close to Danny. "Then who did?"

What the hell was Danny supposed to say? *My sleepwalking girlfriend gutted your partner. It was all a misunderstanding, see, there's this mesmerist...*

Garrett watched Danny struggle. He smiled, almost brotherly. "It's all right. You're going to tell me eventually. Why did you come here? To play in Volpe's private little morgue? Is that what gets you off? You one of his groupies? What's Byron Volpe to you?"

"Nothing, I swear... I came here..." Danny sighed. "I came here to find Laura..."

"Laura who?" Garrett demanded, but it clicked before Danny could answer. "Laura Baxter? The sleeping girl? Oh, this makes perfect sense. *You're the one who kidnapped her.* You were at the hospital tonight—don't say you weren't. You're all over the security footage. But I almost get it. So are you in this with Volpe? Were you there to break him out?"

"No! I went there to-"

"You went there to *what?*"

"I went there to kill him."

Garrett couldn't quite wrap his head around that. For one thing, Volpe was eight feet tall and this kid was a hundred pounds soaking wet. "Why?"

Danny spoke slowly: "Because of Laura. I love her."

Garrett felt very tired. "Son, you are not making any sense at all."

"We've got to help her! Volpe's got her and I think he's going to kill her. He's obsessed with her."

"Oh, *he's* obsessed with her," Garrett said.

Danny talked past him. "I thought he'd be here. But he's not. We have to find him… Please there isn't much time!"

Maybe it was the lack of sleep and the desperate need to piss, but in that moment Garrett felt oddly moved by this clearly damaged kid. He considered lowering his gun.

Then the phone on the desk began to ring.

Garrett's eyes went from the phone to Danny. "You expecting a call?"

"Is that even plugged in?

Garrett didn't want to look down to confirm. He just wanted the ringing to stop. "That's all right, I'll get it."

The phone was black beneath the omnipresent mold. It looked like a crustacean. Garrett lifted the receiver and put it as close to his ear as he could without touching it. "Yeah, you've reached Detective Garrett." In response he got a long quiet hiss. Garrett sighed. "Hello?"

Another pause, but shorter. And the voice that came through was soft and quiet and menacing. "What a pleasant surprise. I was expecting someone else… Someone a bit younger."

"Who is this?" Garrett glanced at Danny and felt another chill. "Volpe?"

(At the sound of the name, Danny's heart dropped into his bowels.)

The voice on the phone oozed pride. "Please call me Byron. You don't happen to be with a young man… a very love sick young man?" Garrett didn't answer. His brain struggled for a snappy response. The voice chuckled at the hesitation. "I see. May I talk to him?"

Garrett shook his head to clear the fog. "You can talk to me."

"Very well," said Volpe, and his voice changed. Still deep and oily and resonant, now he used the voice of the worms: "Then listen to me… I know who you are, Jeff. I know your secrets… I know the dark places that you hide… I know what you do when you are alone…"

Danny couldn't hear Volpe's side of the conversation. He could only watch Garrett's face go slack, almost childlike in its guilt.

"I know your dreams…"

"Dreams?" echoed Garrett.

"Detective, don't listen to him!"

The voice of the worms were soothing, comforting. "It's time to share your dreams."

Danny struggled against his handcuffs. Billy showed him how to get out of them once but his brain wouldn't still for him to accomplish anything. He just wanted to flee.

But Garrett dropped the phone and was on him in a second. Someone else was behind his eyes. "It's time," said Volpe through Garrett. He shoved Danny ahead of him. There was a celebration to attend.

From within her tomb in the wall, the dead girl watched the pair depart. They weren't her rescuers after all.

They'd never even learn her name.

CHAPTER 21

IN THE HELLISH LANDSCAPE OF ASH AND bloodstained sky, Laura found herself standing once again before the Clouded Man's crooked metal house. Instead of fear and despair, Laura felt angry.

Laura was... no, she wouldn't whisper it. Laura was *pissed.*

The sky roiled and fought itself, rumbling and complaining. Laura realized it was the *house* causing the disturbance. The house and the Clouded Man within. It was time to stop this.

With determined steps, Laura marched past the field of rotating mirrors and the gauntlet of giant skeletons. She ignored the faceless things whispering at her in the darkness. It was time to tell the Clouded Man to go away.

Suddenly, the twisted door blew open. The Clouded Man stood howling in the doorway, his branch hair scraping against the frame.

For the first time in her life, Laura said, and *meant*: "I'm not afraid of you!"

The Clouded Man spread his arms to her. They stretched impossibly long, from the doorway, down the path, reaching for her. She refused to run.

Mine! Screamed the thunder. And the Volpe Worm was speeding towards her from the other end of the path. She was trapped between the nightmares. The Clouded Man's sore-ridden arms wrapped around her. Then they became quite familiar.

The hands were strong, even protective. *It was Danny.* She turned and looked up at him. That was his face, right? It was so dark... She returned his hug, squeezing him tight. "It's you..."

All around them, the mirrored plates began to rattle and shake and crack and splinter. The world of ash became a world of *sound.* They were in the eye of a hurricane. A god's tantrum.

The arms around her were no longer comforting. No longer smooth. Scabrous, oozing—

"You're not Danny!"

It was the Clouded Man. It was the Volpe Worm. It was all the nasty filth that ever was. The burning eyes stared into her skull. Vile lips parted to say: "Now I'll show you the truth."

GARRETT SHOVED Danny into the back of his Crown Vic and they drove down to The Docks. Before he knew it, they were at Billy's Studio.

"Why are we here?" Danny demanded. "What does he want? Whatever Volpe is asking you to do, don't do it!"

Unmoved, Garrett parked, came around and dragged Danny from the car. His grip on Danny's shoulder was impossibly strong as he steered the prisoner towards the front door. With a smile, Garrett pushed the doorbell with his elbow. Jenna Jameson's orgasm noise flooded out.

"Don't do this," Danny said to Garrett. He called out, "Billy, don't open the door!"

But in true Billy Dornboss fashion, the door slid open. Billy stuck his head through the opening. His eyelids were drooping, eyes downcast, and he looked sick. Sicker than usual, anyway. Without speaking, he gestured with his head for the pair to enter.

"Shit, Billy."

"I've been waiting for you," Billy said. With Volpe's voice.

Not for the first time that night, Danny wanted to cry.

Billy's mouth moved oddly, the jaw worked up and down as he said, in a strange falsetto. "Hi, Danny! Nice to see you! I'm your friend, Billy!"

Billy cocked his head and blood poured from his ear.

The door slid open fully, revealing Volpe the bloody puppet master, his hand jammed into the back of Billy Dornboss's skull. Of course, he'd had to scoop a lot out to make room for his hand. Billy Dornboss was Volpe's meat puppet, A corpse version of a ventriloquist's dummy.

With a sad smile, Volpe let the Billy Meatpuppet collapse to the floor, robbed of spark and potential. "It's too bad about Mr. Dornboss," Volpe said, staring down at the bloody heap. "I liked him. We shared a lot of the same views. I even liked his art." He glanced around at the room. "Well, some of it anyway."

Garrett manhandled Billy ahead of him and into the depths of The Studio. It had been cleared and re-arranged. Less a studio and now more of a performance space.

"Where's Laura?" Danny demanded.

Volpe laughed. Garrett echoed with his own

high giggle. "Sleeping. She needs her rest. The evening may prove to be very stressful for her."

Volpe moved past them to stand as the Master of Ceremonies. "Detective... I spoke with your mother."

Recognition seemed to spark in Garrett's dull eyes. He was still lost in his own world, but Volpe's voice managed to penetrate. "My mother? What did she say?"

Volpe turned his back on them again as he spoke. "She told me about the little girl down the block. What was her name? Corrine?"

Garrett's head bobbed. "Corrine."

"Corinne's mother knows what happened. It was terrible what you did to her."

"We were just playing. I'm sorry... It... it was an accident."

"I know you were just playing but... I don't think 'I'm sorry' is good enough do you? Not after what you did to her. You'll have to make amends." Volpe turned back and gave Garrett a big warm smile. "You want to, don't you?"

Tears ran down Garrett's face. He seemed grateful for the opportunity. "Yes. Oh, yes." Without another word and gun in hand, Garrett stepped into a shadowy corner of the room to be by himself.

Now it was just the knight and the sorcerer.

"Where is she?" Danny said again.

Volpe stared up at the ceiling, pondering the beams. "We seem to have a problem, you and I. We both want the same thing."

"Fine! Why don't you just use your psychic crap to kill me then she'll be all yours?"

Volpe continued to study the ceiling, but smiled again. "But she won't, you see. She'll think of you. She's found a protector in you. Even in my realm.

Isn't that sad? She'll dream of you like something out of a cheap Gothic novel. I can't have any martyrs. I need to erase you. So that no little fragment, no twinge of something lost is left in her heart. You must be erased in this world and in hers."

Somewhere in the darkness, Danny heard the hammer of Garrett's gun dry click on an empty chamber. Danny suddenly understood what would be required of the detective's amends.

"Why Laura?:

Only then did Volpe look at him. "You know why. She is the most perfect and pure thing that's ever walked this planet. And I... I am the most corrupt. How can it be otherwise?"

Without another word, Volpe shot his hand forward, stabbing a hypodermic into Danny's neck. Whether it was the drug or Volpe, Danny's head filled with images of squirming maggots, all screaming with Laura's voice.

CHAPTER 22

Click!

Desperately, Danny clawed out of unconsciousness. He fought and swam until black became gray became reality.

Click!

He shook his head to clear his vision. The light vanished for a second, then returned. It was merely Garrett passing by, face vacant, eyes haunted. He spun the cylinder of his revolver again. Slapped it closed, held it to his temple. *Click.*

Senses returning, Danny realized his arms were still handcuffed behind him. He would remain a hostage. His mouth was taped shut. No longer would he participate in debate.

Billy's Studio had been transformed. Moldering drapery and old drop cloth had been hung to form something between a cave and a proscenium arch. A performance was being readied for a captive audience of one.

Music swelled behind the curtains. Danny's idiot savant brain recognized it from *Romeo & Juliet,* "Dance of the Knights." Billy had programmed it into an Orchestration Device he'd built but hadn't gotten around to destroying.

The curtains began to move. The players were in place. As the music swelled, the curtains parted. Two of Billy's automatons trundled forward: the top hatted Metal Man with his spinning hypno eyes, and the barely finished Torso Girl, whose arms and legs were mere wireframe, but the breasts had been sculpted with loving detail. They wobbled about and pulled back another drop cloth, revealing Billy's Orchestration: a glass box enclosing a variety of steam-driven instruments. The air made the accordion bellow, the trumpets play, the percussion bang. All to Prokofiev.

Another figure emerged. Danny recognized it as another of Billy's angrily abandoned creations. A sexless mannequin body affixed with a woman's plaster head. Out of her sex-doll mouth protruded a light bulb. It moved to a bank of curtain levers and drew one down.

Again, curtains parted, this time on either side of the stage. Tables had been improvised into risers, upon which on the left, a young brunette with goggles over her eyes, played her cello blindly; and on the right, a girl with white-blonde hair, bowed away at a viola, in perfect accompaniment. If it wasn't so grotesque, it would have been magnificent.

Such a marvelous display of God Volpe's Will.

The Hideous Automaton threw another lever. The lights bloomed and now there were all of Billy's anthropomorphized machines, jerking and bobbing roughly in time with the music. The movements of two young women became jerky, robotic, frenzied, as the music swelled.

In the center of the stage, a final figure was unveiled. A tall figure in a robe, its face a porcelain phrenologist's bust, illustrated with all the elements of the brain. Its face looked exactly like Byron

Volpe. Behind this figure, the Top Hat and Torso Girl turned cranks and began the Danse Macabre.

With a flourish, the Volpe figure covered its face with a black fan, then made a slicing motion with a knife across the obstructed throat. The fan flipped, revealing the head completely missing.

Hidden gears whirled. A simple black box rose into place at the figure's side. Slowly, the lid raised, and with it came the transported porcelain white head of Volpe, its burning eyes now quite dead.

The visage cracked. Mechanics clicked. The Volpe face split into thirds and opened like hideous flower petals, revealing the face of a stillborn baby beneath.

With a shudder and creak, the box lid closed again, now capped with the eye-in-the-pyramid symbol best associated with Aleister Crowley. (Or the one-dollar bill.) (*What is the Eye of Providence?*") What it all meant, Danny had no idea.

The music crashed in crescendo and the girls dropped like discarded marionettes. They seemed quite dead. Had they been animated by Volpe's will alone? Was he really that powerful?

As the music faded, all of the mechanical wonders wound down. Top Hat fell clattering to the ground. Bits of gears and machinery spewed out to a mechanical wheezing sound. The Torso Woman stopped moving.

Volpe turned and gave a little shrug. "Ah well, if Mr. Dornboss was still with us I would recommend *The Modern Engineer, Technical Press 1938. Chapter five, Issues of Reliability in Modern Machines.*"

For a large man, Volpe could move quickly. He seemed to materialize behind Danny, digging his chin into the young man's shoulder. "Sorry about the rather conventional restraints… I have to stay focused… and the night's young."

Volpe glanced up and the two girls sprang back into position, ready for instructions. "Young ladies, the piece that you've be practicing so hard... play it."

The human automatons ended their jerky movements and settled in to their learned routine to play *Jupiter*.

Volpe sighed in contentment. "Lovely... Now to business. I think we can talk frankly, don't you?"

Swearing under his breath, Danny worked his hands against the cuffs. He felt Volpe's heavy hand on the top of his head.

"Don't do that. I'd hate to have to do something overt and vengeful. You must love your fate, which is your life." Volpe leaned forward and licked the side of Danny's face. Danny recoiled, then twisted to stare Volpe in the eye.

Anger flashed across Volpe's face, then it resumed its amused mask. "Brave of you to look me in the eye. Not many who've done that have survived. Gaze into the abyss too long... and the abyss will gaze into you. *Tick, Tick, Tick, Tick, Tick.*"

Standing straight, Volpe stepped forward then turned back, arms spread, the Master of Ceremonies. "And now *Paradise Lost*: Our exquisite lost angel. Our Peacock Angel."

Again, the mechanicals came to life while the two dead girls slid into *Jupiter*'s next movement. Above them all, the rafters seemed to shudder.

Amidst the creaking of pulleys, a coffin lined with white satin slowly descended from the ceiling. The lid lifted and revealed Volpe's "angel."

Shocked but not surprised, Danny saw that the angel was Laura Baxter. Her alabaster face was serene in sleep, her lithe body draped in gauzy silk. Affixed to her back were wings made of peacock feathers, origin unknown. Her angel wings.

Jesus, she's beautiful.

Volpe's voice spoiled the elegant display. "There are only two worthwhile things in life... danger and play. And what more dangerous plaything than a woman?"

With that, the next act of the tableau. Laura's body rose from the coffin, wired to a harness. She hung suspended in the air, bare legs and feet hanging limp. With a hideous intimacy, Volpe caressed one wing. Carelessly, he plucked a feather. The needle-thin tip came away dripping blood.

Her suspended body turned in a circle, displaying Volpe's hard work. The beautiful feathered wings, so blue and bright, had been sewn directly into Laura's back. (*Danny thought then of the nurse at the hospital, stitching away at her own face.*) The stitching had been clean. The only blood streamed from the wound left behind where Volpe removed the needled plume. The wings that defined her now were permanent.

"Laura, it's time to dream," Volpe hissed. "Stand. Stand."

On cue, Laura opened her eyes. Immediately, they found Danny.

The angel thrashed in rage. Volpe turned and tried to hold her gaze.

Desperate to get free, Danny tried to scream her name, but the tape sealed his mouth. He twisted his wrists against the tight cuffs. He thought about breaking his thumb—more than willing to do it. He could feel blood drip between his fingers.

"It's all right," Volpe whispered to Laura. "You're going to see clearly now. You will finally see the truth. And you will know that this dream," he motioned to Danny and the real world, "is not for you."

Laura's eyes fluttered, the trance taking hold. Volpe was letting the worms out.

"I've always protected you."

The blood made the cuffs slick. Danny's hand was almost free.

Laura's head dipped forward, loose on her neck.

Free! Danny ripped the tape from his mouth. "Laura! Fight him!"

He meant to say more. He wanted to scream encouragement and strength. But he felt something grab his head from the inside and hold his tongue flat.

He felt worms in his brain. They took away his body. All he could do was scream. But not out loud. Danny's legs buckled and he dropped to his knees. He felt invisible hands claw at his head, pulling it back to face his accuser and his judge.

Somewhere in the dark, he heard another *Click!*

"Detective," Volpe said, "why don't you put it in your mouth next time?"

LAURA... *open your eyes.*

The voice was Danny's. No... the voice was Volpe disguised as Danny.

Laura could see herself suspended between the Land of Ash and Dannyland. Only Dannyland was now just as violent. The chaos of The Clouded Man mirrored in Volpe's torture of Danny.

Mirrors...

She'd had enough.

Laura... open your eyes.

Doing so, Laura left the Land of Ash for the last time.

Doing so, Laura's eyes opened and brought her into Dannyland. No...

This wasn't Dannyland. This was Danny's nightmare. He was dreaming that she was dreaming *him*.

There was searing pain in her back—there was no pain in Lauraland, and only fear in the Land of Ash. In Dannyland there were fluffy doggies (and perverts) and ice cream (and screaming). This *was* Danny's nightmare.

"No..." said the whisper in her head, the one that sounded like both Danny and the worms. "This is your clouded man... look at him. This is the thing that haunts your world... our world."

Volpe stepped forward, as if stepping out of his own voice and into Danny's reality. He smiled at Danny. "Don't you think you should say something to her?" He held up his hand before Danny's face, fingers together, tongue gesticulating, as if operating a (*Billy Dornboss*) puppet.

Danny felt his mouth open and close. Volpe jerked his hand at the wrist. Danny dropped to all fours. He couldn't fight it. He could only concentrate on breathing. Volpe wasn't concerned about his plaything's petty need for oxygen. Every muscle in his body fought against Volpe's control, but the worms just laughed.

Danny could hear them in his head. They said, in Volpe's voice:

"Tell her what you really think of her, Dan." The voice was in his ears and in his head and all around. "Tell her what's in your heart... Share it so will all know."

As Volpe's lips move, so do Danny's. *Shitty ventriloquist!*

But Danny heard his voice spill from his mouth. "You are..." It sounded like him, but *not* like him. Like a ventriloquist's impression of him. Insult upon insult. "You are..." Danny felt his head jerk up, forcing him to look Laura in the eye. "...*nothing* to me."

Tears filled Laura's eyes. The words tore at her.

"I took you because you were easy..." Danny snarled, his voice filled with hatred. "You were a stupid doll that I could dress up... How do you think I could care about somebody... *something* like you?" Danny's own tears stung his eyes, and they pleaded with her not to listen. "I'm done with you."

Before any more tears could fall, the torture was interrupted by an impossibly loud *BANG!*

Detective Garrett's luck finally ran out. Perhaps now his amends could be considered made.

The gunshot did more than startle Laura. The noise somehow freed her. She was more awake than she'd ever been, fully aware of her surroundings.

This wasn't a dream. It wasn't Danny's. It wasn't hers.

This is what *real life* was. This is where Volpe really lived.

In a place of pain and anger and confusion. Worse than hospital. This *real world* didn't want to help anyone. It wouldn't even pretend.

Laura felt behind her, searching for whatever was holding her so painfully in mid-air, fingers probing the sore stitching keeping the wings in place.

Volpe's attention was away from her, more entertained with his psychosomething torture. All he wanted to do was hurt. Hurt her. Hurt Danny. Hurt *everyone*. She didn't understand it and she didn't (*goddamn*) care!

"I despise you," Danny said in Volpe's voice. "The sight of you makes me ill."

Tears streamed down his begging eyes. Laura watched as things broke inside him.

"Ohhhh," moaned Volpe through Danny. The sorcerer turned and faced his angel, reaching out to stroke the tears from her cheeks. "Don't cry," he said in his own voice, leaving Danny now to move his lips silently. "I'll be here for you always... 'If he loved you with all the depth of his soul for a thousand years, he couldn't love you as much as I do in a single day.'"

(*Emily Bronte*, struggled Danny's dying brain. "*What is 'Wuthering Heights'?*")

Triumphant, Volpe the Victor took his prize. He leaned forward, glistening mouth wide, tongue slithering over his teeth, his mouth enveloped Laura's. He could taste the tears on her tongue.

In her head, she heard: "You will love me... I will *make* you."

As he pulled away, a gleam of crimson caught Volpe's eye. A drip of blood upon Laura's flawless foot...

Laura leaned close and whispered in his ear, "Then you will only be loving yourself."

She didn't know how many of the foot-long needle plumes she'd ripped from her back. Laura only hoped she'd gotten enough—as she drove the bundle into Volpe's throat. They pierced through his lower jaw and impaled his tongue. When he opened his mouth to scream, blood jettisoned from his throat.

It was enough to break Danny free from the worms.

In a rage, Danny the Knight seized a weapon—a heavy hydraulic pipe—and fell upon the sorcerer. With a viciousness that almost shocked him, Danny beat the creature mercilessly. His breath caught each time a bone broke beneath that pipe.

After several strikes, Volpe's shouts of outrage and agony turned to uncontrollable laughter.

Danny put his weight into his next few blows, but only managed to knock the wind out of the giant.

His voice was a bloody gurgle, "Is that it?" He was on his knees, bleeding from every hole in his head. "I thought you had more in you than that," the sorcerer gasped. "You know I'll still have her. They'll patch me up, lock me away someplace... and I'll make sure Sleeping Beauty is in the next room." His smile was the most hideous. "Just like last time."

The sorcerer gave it one last go. With his last surge of strength, he let loose the worms.

Danny's arm went slack. The pipe dropped from his grasp.

All that was left for Volpe to do was order him to happily, cheerfully, *stop breathing.* Volpe's lips parted—

Then his eyes burst inwards, impaled upon a mismatched pair of screwdrivers, driven home by Laura. Driven home by rage.

"No, you won't! *No You Won't!*" she howled, putting all of her weight behind the tool handles, driving them as far into Volpe's skull as she could. There were two cracking *pops* as she pierced bone. "I'm never going back! I'm staying here in *this* dream... Forever and ever and ever!"

Blinded, Volpe thrashed his arms in the air, but Laura evaded his grasp. With a final primal shout, she kicked her bare foot into Volpe's chest. The sorcerer fell back in a bloody heap, fingers clawing the air. Volpe coughed a gout of gore. Bloody fingerprints on the tops of the screwdrivers gave Volpe an almost comical pop-eyed look. Maybe in a million years they could laugh about it. From a sitting position, he gurgled his last: "That was good... that was the one..."

Slowly, he laid back, his evil and power seeping

away as his heart slowed and brain stopped. "We're not done here…" His words trailed off, but his lips continued to move silently.

Danny would never be certain, but it seemed as if Volpe were trying to say, "Tick, tick…ti…" But the sorcerer ran down.

With the last of her strength, Laura ripped the wings from her back. Her exhausted mind barely registered the pain. Her ears didn't hear her blood spattering the floor. Unsteady on her feet, she wobbled a little. Danny caught her.

"No, no, don't fall asleep. We have to get out of here. The police are going to show up and we can't be here." He got his arms around her and gave her an encouraging shake. "Come on, Laura… don't fall asleep."

Somewhere in the distance, maybe as far as tomorrow, sirens lied that help was coming. Sleep fought her, and so much of her own fight was gone. Though she tried her hardest, her legs stopped wanting to move. *Stay awake! Stay awake!*

They reached the door. She tried to help but now her arms didn't want to work. Danny shifted her weight and reached for the knob and freedom.

A heavy hand gripped Danny's shoulder and spun him around. Laura dropped to the ground, still fighting sleep. Garrett had survived his game of Russian Roulette. Half of his lower jaw was gone, teeth shattered, ear missing, eye socket hollow and wet. "I have a message from Volpe…" Garrett said, half in his voice, half in that of Volpe's ghost. "Tick. Tick. Tick. Tick,. Tick!"

BANG!

Danny tried to turn but the bullet hit the back of his skull. He dropped like a trapdoor weight.

The force of the blast threw Garrett backwards,

the last of Volpe's will vanishing in the impact. The sorcerer had the final say.

Laura's cry was pure anguish. "*No!*" She cried and gathered up Danny's body, felt his blood spill across her lap. She sobbed and rocked him. "No... No... I love you. Please don't leave me... I can't bear to live without you.... I can't be here alone."

Danny's eyes fluttered. They moved independently.

Laura couldn't comprehend it. They'd been forced out of Danny's dream. Maybe she could bring him to Lauraland. Or maybe they could dream someplace better. "Come on... We can... We can.. We can dream... let's dream... let's dream forever. Let's just *dream that we're dreaming.*"

It took just a second to find a comfortable position, with Danny's head on her arm, their faces nearly touching.

If she heard the sirens blaring, the door kicked in, the cops shouting, she didn't let on. Or else she didn't care. She let sleep take her.

Them.

She dreamed that they got up off the floor. Danny was healed and healthy and they were both happy. She dreamed that they moved hand-in-hand to the door, where all the policemen waved and the sun was shining.

She dreamed that Danny smiled at her and said, "It's a beautiful day."

EPILOGUE

Dr. Corso finished his story. His interviewer turned off the little tape recorder and stared back at the physician in stunned silence.

Finally, Phil shook his head and remembered his purpose. "And Volpe. He's dead, right?"

Dr. Corso nodded. Yes. He's quite dead.

So was Dr. Bhyle, Nurse Sarah, a security guard, several orderlies, not to mention the people on the team Bhyle had deemed unworthy of introduction… more corpses than the end of Romeo and Juliet.

"What about the girl… Laura Baxter?"

"Maybe it would be easier if I just show you."

It was just a short trip across the room, to an area secured behind a privacy sheet. "She's here…"

Phil hesitated. "In the Morgue?"

"Again, she's alive. We moved her here to keep her away from prying eyes, and to sustain her. It's part of a new therapy."

"What about Danny Sloan? Is he alive?"

Tired of repeating himself, Dr. Corso pulled the sheet aside. There it was, the Sleepers' Tank. Filled to the brim with a special oxygenated fluid to aerate the tissues, looking very much like Thurston's Crystal Cage or Houdini's Drowning

Tank. The highest technology masquerading as magic.

Corso flipped a switch on a side panel. The tank lit up inside with a pale blue glow—

—illuminating the nude bodies of Laura and Danny, floating peacefully next to each other. Sleeping swimmers. They held hands, fingers entwined. Tranquil in their dreamy dance.

"I thought I should keep them together."

Phil stood transfixed, sharing their blue glow. "Will they ever wake up?

Dr. Corso shrugged. "I don't know." He wanted another cigarette but he'd already broken enough rules. "Daniel is in a coma and I don't think he can. Laura hasn't woken since that night..." His smile was sad. "Maybe she doesn't want to." He gave the young man a few seconds before pointedly looking at his watch.

Phil didn't move. "Doc. Would it be alright if I just stay here for a minute..."

Dr. Corso nodded. He didn't care. He doubted anyone else would. His little experiment cost the hospital a fortune but they were content to ignore it in the wake of the scandal of murder and mayhem. The Sleepers were in their basement dwelling and were best forgotten about.

Corso thought about the fresh pack of cigars in his glove compartment and left the strange man to his captive audience.

Once alone—more or less—Phil took up his little briefcase and laid it out on a little supply table. Unpacking the case, he set up the portable record player. It took him a second to find an outlet, then had to fuss with the table to get it closer, cursing the too-short cord. Finally, he had his presentation together.

Reaching into his satchel, he pulled out a 45 rpm

record, holding it by the edges like it was the original Holy Grail and he wasn't about to let his filthy
fingers defile it. Carefully, he slid it from its paper
sleeve and into its rightful place on the spindle.
Reverently, he switched on the player and dropped
the needle.

"I always keep a promise," he said to Floating
Danny. The warm hum of vinyl preceded the
opening notes of the song. "The Bossmen on Lucky
Eleven Records, 1966," he said.

*"You're the girl for meeee. Hey, hey, I want you to
know / How much I love you so / I'll never let go / You're
the one for meee."*

Phil hoped the music gave them pleasant
dreams.

Outside the Mulliner House, the day is bright
and warm and sunny.

Eight year old Danny and Laura walk hand-in-
hand down the stairs towards the open door.
Summer is waiting for them.

It's always summer in LauraDannyLand. And
today, there's music.

Little girl Laura gives Little Boy Danny a kiss.
"It *is* a beautiful day."

Tomorrow, they'll dream an even better one.

IMAGE GALLERY

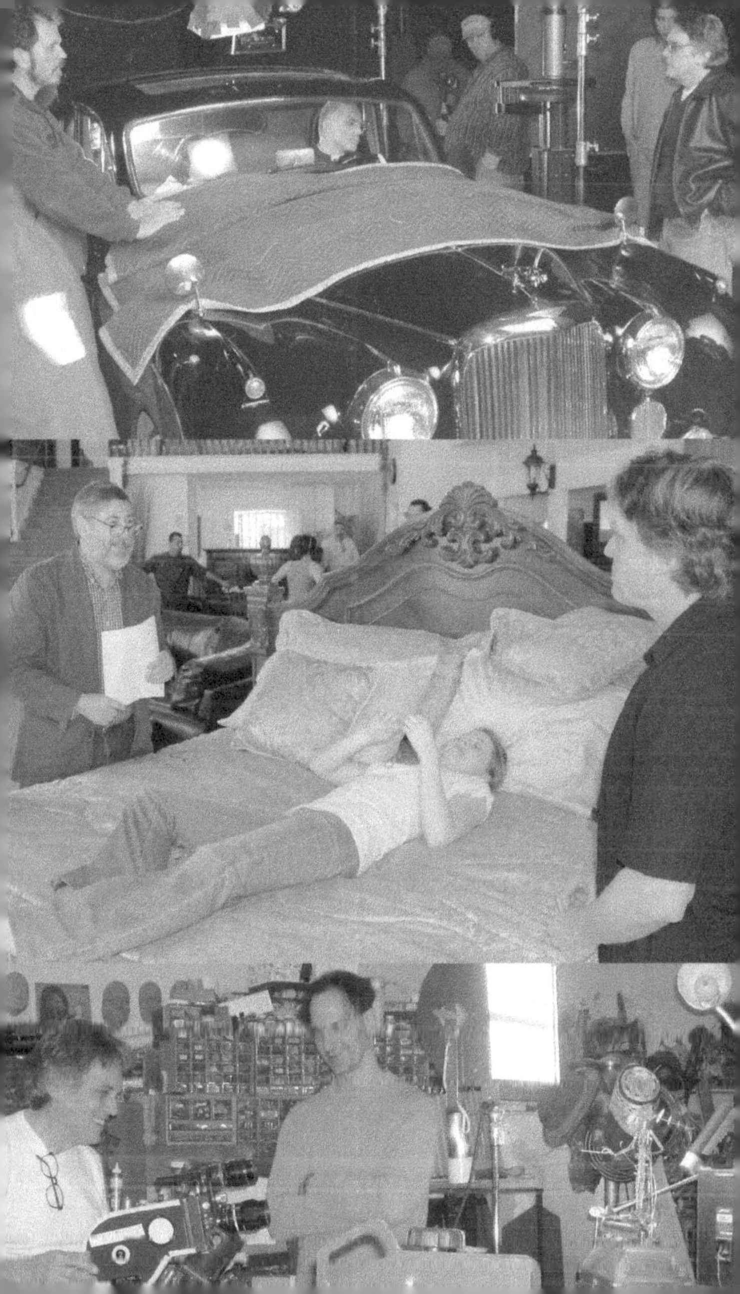

How Long Do You
Have To Live?

ROLL
SCENE
PROD 44003
X160
Director WILLIAM WILLIAMS
Camera CHRISTIAN SCHROEDER
Date 11/20/05
MOS D/N
18

PARASOMNIA

RISING STORM PRODUCTIONS presents
William Malone's
PARASOMNIA
Starring
DYLAN PURCELL CHERILYN WILSON JEFFREY COMBS TIMOTHY BOTTOMS DOV TIFFENBACH
with SEAN YOUNG and PATRICK KILPATRICK as Byron Volpe
Visual Effects Supervisor GENE WARREN III Production Designer KATHERINE G. VALLIN
Conceptual Art ZDZISLAW BEKSINSKI Edited by ANTHONY ADLER
Music by NICHOLAS PIKE Cinematography by CHRISTIAN SEBALDT
Produced by JANE HAMILTON Executive Producers JON J. JANNOTTA WILLIAM MALONE
Written and Directed by WILLIAM MALONE

THE RETRO MASS MARKET COLLECTION

COLLECT THEM ALL!

- ☐ HELLRAISER: THE TOLL
- ☐ FRIGHT NIGHT
- ☐ RE-ANIMATOR
- ☐ HARDCORE
- ☐ WISHMASTER
- ☐ HELLRAISER: BLOODLINE
- ☐ TITAN FIND
- ☐ CREATURE
- ☐ VAMP
- ☐ SCARED TO DEATH
- ☐ OF UNKNOWN ORIGIN
- ☐ MANBORG
- ☐ ATTACK OF THE KILLER TOMATOES
- ☐ THE SPECIAL
- ☐ TAMARA
- ☐ FORBIDDEN ZONE
- ☐ COURAGE UNDER FIRE
- ☐ LONG WEEKEND
- ☐ THE ODD JOB
- ☐ BLUE SUNSHINE
- ☐ THE ONLY HOUSE
- ☐ SQUIRM
- ☐ CRUEL JAWS
- ☐ SPLICE
- ☐ THE PIT/TEDDY
- ☐ THE PIKE
- ☐ THE BEAST OF KANE
- ☐ THE TUXEDO WARRIOR

- ☐ LIFE CYCLE
- ☐ CHOPPING MALL
- ☐ ALL THROUGH THE HOUSE
- ☐ CHRISTMAS WITH THE DEAD
- ☐ VIRUS: HELL OF THE LIVING DEAD
- ☐ RATS: NIGHT OF TERROR
- ☐ PLAN 9 FROM OUTER SPACE
- ☐ DEADGIRL
- ☐ SLEEPAWAY CAMP
- ☐ BETRAYAL AND BLACK LACE
- ☐ SPIDER BABY
- ☐ RETURN OF THE LIVING DEAD 3
- ☐ LUST FOR A VAMPIRE
- ☑ PARASOMNIA
- ☐ PALE RIDER*
- ☐ THE GAUNTLET*
- ☐ MURDER BY PHONE*
- ☐ REDNECK ZOMBIES*
- ☐ NIGHT OF THE DEMON*
- ☐ RETRIBUTION*
- ☐ OLD HENRY*
- ☐ CUBE*
- ☐ UTTER TRASH*

*Coming Soon